HONESTY
& Ahmad

DAK

Royalty Publishing House is now accepting manuscripts from aspiring or experienced urban romance authors!

WHAT MAY PLACE YOU ABOVE THE REST:

Heroes who are the ultimate book bae: strong-willed, maybe a little rough around the edges but willing to risk it all for the woman he loves.

Heroines who are the ultimate match: the girl next door type, not perfect - has her faults but is still a decent person. One who is willing to risk it all for the man she loves.

The rest is up to you! Just be creative, think out of the box, keep it sexy and intriguing!

If you'd like to join the Royal family, send us the first 15K words (60 pages) of your completed manuscript to submissions@royaltypublishing-house.com

Synopsis

*H*ow can someone so beautiful live a life so ugly? Honesty is a troubled young lady trying to survive. She's trying to take care of her sister while her mother is battling cancer. She will do any and everything to get money, even if it means taking things that don't belong to her. But what happens when she takes from the wrong person and falls in love with the right person? When Honesty's mother dies, she is left with the world on her shoulders. With a best friend like Naomi, who lives like there is no tomorrow, she finds herself in some trouble.

Ahmad is the man of the streets, and he crosses paths with Honesty. After witnessing all that she's been through, he proves to her that he's down for her and willing to be at war with almost anyone for a girl he barely knows. After giving her a lifestyle that she dreams of she betrays his trust, and it's too much for him to bear. Honesty learns quickly that for every action, there is an equal and opposite reaction.

Prologue

"I gotta get my baby back," Honesty mumbled as she squirmed from under the man who had fallen asleep on her and weighed about 250 pounds.

It had been almost a year since she had last seen her baby sister Hannah. She had no idea how she was doing, and she felt foolish. She had up and left her baby sister without a word. She knew that Ms. G was taking the best care of her because she always did. She treated Honesty and Hannah like her own children.

She looked around the abandoned apartment, and for the first time, she was disgusted with what she saw. This was the first time that she was sober in a long time. She had grown accustomed to getting high and letting it be her escape, but there was no escaping it at that very moment. She sat up on the bed that was on the floor and looked at the John that she had just finished fucking. She was ready to get out of dodge. The bando wasn't what it had once been for her. At first, it was fun and gave her an adrenaline rush because of the high. But she had gotten so used to the drug. It didn't take her to the places that it once had.

First, she needed to get her best friend Naomi. She threw on the dingy white shorts that she had been wearing for the past month and slipped on the black slippers that were once white. She tiptoed through the warehouse looking for Naomi. She knew she was in there somewhere. She walked to the back room and saw a small silhouette on the floor and tiptoed over to the person. She turned the lamp on so she could get a better view. With every step and action she took, it seemed like she held her breath. She didn't want to get caught trying to escape the place she once loved but now hated. She removed the hair from the face of the person lying down and saw it was Naomi.

"Nay, get up. We gotta go," she whispered while nudging her best friends' body. "Nay, let's go. Mommy here to get us," she continued to lie in a whisper.

She knew her best friend was high, but she was trying to get the fuck out without being noticed. At first, being there had been a choice, but over time, it was like they had gotten so deeply involved that they no longer owned themselves. She pushed her off her side and onto her back to only see a syringe hanging from her arm.

"No, no, no, no, no!" she yelled in panic. "Nay, we gotta go," she said with her voice cracking and tears falling from her face.

She pulled out the syringe and shook her, but Nay was unresponsive. She knew she was gone but didn't want to face the reality of it.

This wasn't what she imagined. She had thought they would actually make it out alive, get clean, and live the life they had once lived. Her stomach twisted and turned into knots. She just cried, releasing all the pain she'd been through over the years. She picked herself up with the tears still falling from her eyes. This was a wakeup call for her. She had to find her baby sister and Ahmad and get away from all of this. She wasn't fully clean, but she knew Ahmad wouldn't mind helping her. Even with all the drugs she had been using, he still loved her the same way he had loved her the minute they met.

She walked back into the living room, and the John was still laid out on the floor. The blowjob she gave him was elite. She sucked his dick until it couldn't get hard anymore. She walked over to his pants that were on the floor and put her hand into his pocket. She grabbed the wad of money and cell phone that was inside.

Before she knew it, he was grumbling and turning over. Like a deer in headlights, she froze while holding her breath. She got low to the ground, pretending she was sleep too. He looked over to her and grabbed a fistful of her hair. Without warning, he shoved his dick into her mouth. She cringed but still sucked his penis so he could go back to sleep.

"Yeah, baby. Right there. Let me feel that throat," he said, stuffing himself down her throat until he couldn't anymore.

Honesty was trying to be cooperative and not do anything to set him off as she did her thing. She just had to put him to sleep for a little longer. When she felt his body tense up, she knew he was about to cum. She tried to pull her head up so her hands could finish off the job, but his hand forced the back of her head down. The harder she tried to put her head up the harder he pushed down.

He pushed down so hard that her face became suffocated in the fat on his stomach. She let go of his dick and scrambled, trying to get free from him, but it was no use.

He kept pumping in and out of her even after he nutted. Honesty tried reaching under her pillow where she kept a sharp piece of glass. Once her fingers touched it, she grabbed it and stabbed him in his side with it.

"Aghhhh! Stupid bitch!" he yelled while finally letting her head free.

Honesty sat up, choking on cum and trying to catch her breath. Tears formed in her eyes again. She was tired of being used and taken advantage of. She looked at him as he tried to put pressure on his wound. She wanted to cut his dick off right there, but she knew he would overpower her with his own weight.

"You stupid crackhead bitch! I'mma fucking kill you!" he yelled while tying a shirt around his wound and reaching for her. Honesty swiftly used the sharp glass and went across his face, giving him a buck fifty.

She stood on her two feet and made a run for it. As soon as she reached outside, the light from the sun slightly blinded her. Before her eyes could adjust, she heard a gunshot behind her. She took off running down the street without knowing exactly where she was going. She just wanted to get out of sight. She pulled out the phone she had taken and dialed the only number she remembered with hopes that Ahmad would answer his phone when she needed him the most.

* * *

AHMAD SAT across from Hannah as they both ate their breakfast. Every day, she began to look more and more like Honesty. Something in him just wished Honesty could see how much she had grown. But with the drugs she was on, he knew she would never see what he saw.

"I miss Honesty. I can't understand why she just won't come home," Hannah said, putting her fork down.

"It's easy for us to say for her to come home, but it's not easy for her to actually come," he explained.

Before Hannah could respond, a call came through to his phone from a number he didn't really know. He thought of not answering, but out of curiosity, he did.

"Ahmad," Honesty said through the phone. Her voice was like music to his ears. His heart began beating like a drum.

"Ahmad," she spoke again. He so badly wanted to say something back, but his words were caught in his throat.

"Where are you?" he asked as he rose out of his seat and grabbed his car keys. Hannah was right on his tail. She knew it was her older sister on the line.

"Ms. Grandberry's house. Nay's gone." She sobbed into the phone. She couldn't believe that her best friend was really gone.

"Stay there, and I'll be there in a second," Ahmad said, hanging up the phone and speeding to get his girl back.

Honesty

One Year Prior

"*H*onesty, that nigga Jayce throwing a party at Sue's tonight. We in there!" my best friend Naomi yelled.

"I don't know about all that 'cause my mama ain't feeling too well, and I don't wanna leave Hannah alone."

Naomi sucked her teeth. "You never wanna go out nowhere," she mumbled.

"I do be wanting to go out. I just can't. I don't have it all together like you do," I said while mixing up the oatmeal I had made for my mother. I walked out the kitchen with Naomi on my tail.

"You know your mama won't mind. After she eats dinner, she gon' be sleep."

I walked into my mother's room and straight to her bed. Her cancer was coming back, and she was always in pain, a pain that I just wished I could take from her.

"Ma," I said softly before taking a seat at the edge of her bed.

"Yes, baby?" she said weakly while opening her eyes to look at me. Her eyes seemed so heavy like she was struggling to open them.

"I made you oatmeal, Mommy." She gave me a weak smile.

"Thank you, baby."

It hurt me so much to see her like that. I just couldn't wait for her to get better again and beat cancer for the second time. I fed her the oatmeal slowly, and she ate in silence.

I loved my mother more than life itself. There wasn't a thing she wouldn't do for me and Hannah. Ever since her battle with cancer, she had been going to work off and on. She couldn't work, and I was worried about how I'd get some money to pay the rent and buy some food for us since we were running low. By going to that party, I could snatch me up a honey and get some money out of him.

"I'll go with you tonight, but you gotta give me clothes to wear," I whispered to Naomi.

I rose from the bed and began walking out of my mom's room quietly. She had fallen asleep, and I really didn't want to disturb her.

Naomi followed me back to the kitchen. "Yay. What made you change your mind?"

"Come on, Nay. If anybody knows my situation, it's you. I need to get some money fast." Naomi nodded her head. She knew what was on my mind already.

* * *

WE SAT in the twenty-one and older section of the packed club. Our fake IDs came in clutch. I was confident about the way I looked. These strippers had nothing on me. I was sure I could do this with ease.

I had on a romper that my ass hung out of. I was feeling sexy, and niggas couldn't keep their hands off me. Naomi did my makeup, so I knew I looked good. She braided my hair into one fish braid down my back.

I looked across the club and made eye contact with some dude. He looked like he could be Idris Elba's twin except he had a full beard. My pussy began throbbing at the sight of him. Before I knew it, someone was wrapping their hands around my waist. There was some corny looking dude. I could tell from the ice on his wrist and necklace he wore that he had money. He was already drunk, so all I had to do was get him somewhere private.

"Let me take you home," he whispered into my ear.

"Let me buy you a drink first," I offered. "Two glasses of Henny. Put it on his tab," I said after realizing I didn't have money to spend.

The bartender made the drinks and set it on the table. I rubbed my ass on his print as I slipped a roofie in his drink and stirred it with my finger and turned around to face him. He bodied his drink in three seconds as I sipped mine. He took my drink from my hand and downed it too.

"I don't think we gonna make it to your house, so show me where your car is," I said into his ear seductively. I knew in a minute he was gonna be out like a light. He staggered and walked out the exit, pulling out his car keys. He dropped them, and I picked it up. I pressed the alarm so I could know which car was his as he began to put all his weight on my shoulders. I was just glad the car was close.

Once we got in, I pulled his pants down and began sucking on his itty-bitty dick. In less than a minute, he busted a nut, and I couldn't be happier. I pulled a wipe out of my clutch, wiping my hands and cleaning him up. I looked up at him, and he was knocked out. I dug into his pockets, finding two rolls of money with rubber bands on them. I couldn't be happier at that moment. I put his car keys back in his pocket before hopping out and walking back into the club.

Ahmad

I watched from the back as she reentered the club. I just shook my head at the nigga she walked out with. I was pretty sure she gave him a run for his money literally. There was something about her that made a nigga dig her. Maybe it was that seductive look in her eyes that she didn't know she had.

I watched as she swayed her hips and looked for another victim. She had a rare look. A look of innocence, something I was sure she was far from. She looked lost in her own skin. Just by staring at her, I could see all her insecurities. With the way she pulled her romper down every time it rose up her ass, I could tell it wasn't hers. With the ways niggas was coming at her, trying to buy her drink after drink, I could tell she was on a mission.

Every nigga in here was her prey. I couldn't help but stare at her. I was sure that without the makeup she looked even better. I walked toward her as she leaned with her back to the bar. She was eyeing every nigga who was throwing a month's rent at the strippers.

I stood beside her and looked in the same direction she was looking in. She was eyeing Jay; the nigga was flaunting all the money he had all because he was hosting this. He didn't even know he was being watched.

"You won't be able to get him the way you got the other nigga. If you do get him, he'll be looking for you." She turned around to face me and almost dropped her drink.

"I don't know what you talking about," she said, shrugging her shoulders.

I chuckled to myself. "I ain't tryna knock your hustle or anything, but I been watching you for the past thirty minutes."

She walked away from me, and I just watched her. She walked over to some random nigga and began making conversation. These niggas had no clue what they were getting themselves into. They were getting pimped out by a youngin', and it was definitely amusing. I mean, everyone had to get it by any means necessary.

Around three, I left the club. Shit was starting to get wack, and them tired ass strippers weren't doing their thing. I hopped into my Benz and made my way to Tiana's house. Tiana was my ex that I couldn't leave alone. She had the best pussy I had ever been in.

Ten minutes later, I hopped out my car and opened her door with the key I had always had. Tiana lived in the 'jects with her son Quan.

I walked through the door, and her house was a complete mess. It was nothing new. It was one of the reasons we weren't together. She didn't know how to clean shit up, and I couldn't sleep in a dirty house.

I stepped over the pizza boxes and turned the light on, and the roaches began scattering. I shook my head, walking straight into her bedroom without turning another damn light switch. I knew if I turned on another light, I was gonna walk my ass out the door. I just needed some pussy, and then I was gonna be on my way.

I turned her room light on, and her room was how it had been for the past two months—clothes everywhere. I smacked her on the ass, and it jiggled as she moaned.

"Wake your ass up, Tee." I kicked my boots off and sat them on a chair. I didn't wanna leave and take any unwanted guests with me home.

I pulled out my dick and slapped it on her ass. It was almost as if she smelled dick. Her eyes shot open, and she went straight to daddy and covered him with her warm mouth. I put my hand on the back of her head and forced it down her throat. She didn't even gag, and that's what I loved about her. Most bitches couldn't take nine inches down their throat. She bobbed her head until I nutted in her mouth. She swallowed it all and licked my dick clean. I slipped on a condom and slid into her pussy. She opened and closed her walls while I thrusted.

"Yes, daddy! Right there!" she said in between moans.

I pushed her legs up to her head, and I felt myself about to nut. I pulled out, and she pulled off the condom and began to suck my dick until I nutted.

I nutted in her mouth a second time and caught my breath. She got up off the bed and gave me a wet rag to wipe my dick with. I stuck it back in my pants and began to get dressed again.

"Oh, so you only want me for pussy? Next time, don't bring your ass over here. Go to one of them other bitches you fucking. See if they gon' fuck you like I do," she complained.

I just ignored her as I put my boots on. I took out two hundred-dollar bills and set it on her dresser before walking out. She followed me to the door talking her shit, and I tuned her out as always. It was nothing new, and everything she was saying went in one ear and out the other, it didn't move me one bit. I couldn't do nothing but shake my head. Tiana was a headache. That was another reason we couldn't be together. She nagged too damn much.

I walked out her door and out her building. As soon as I walked out the door, shorty walked into me head first. It was the same girl from the club.

"Sorry," she said, avoiding eye contact with me.

"What's your name?" I asked her. I had to get this girl. She was young, but there was something about her that made me want to take her with me.

"Honesty." The name fit her face, but the personality didn't match.

"Ahmad," I said, introducing myself.

She looked into my eyes, and I looked into hers. Then I saw it. It was the eye of a tiger. At least that was what I called it. That was a rare look for females; it was a look most niggas on the street had. It was a look that I had. The tiger's eye was a look of focus, determination, coldness, and fierceness. It was a "get up and get a bag instead of waiting for a bag to come to you" look. I definitely wanted to know her. I was pretty sure she lived around here, so I was sure I'd see her again.

She broke our eye contact and looked down. "Excuse me," she said, and I stepped out her way.

I knew we would meet again, and next time, I would be ready.

Honesty

"*A*liza, Mariah, Zahir, Lyric..." the teacher called out while taking attendance. I had been at this school for a month, and I was already annoyed.

"Honesty…" she called out, and I raised my hand. She looked up and marked me down.

After she took her attendance, she began teaching her lesson. We were in the twelfth grade, and she was teaching eighth grade English. I was pretty sure I was in the wrong class. I flipped to the back of my notebook and began drawing. I had no idea who I was drawing, but whoever that person was, it wasn't me. The person I was drawing knew happiness—something I knew nothing about. Before I could finish shading, the teacher slammed her hand down on my book. She had the wrong kid.

"I'd be wrong if I smacked the shit out you, right?" I said in annoyance.

"Excuse me?" she said with her hands on her chest like my response had surprised her. The entire class stared on and added to her embarrassment. "Go to the office now!" she yelled.

Teachers had shit fucked up. They took their job way too seriously. The only reason I came to school was so that they wouldn't call ACS. My mama was fighting cancer, and I was left to take care of my little sister Hannah. At the age of eighteen, instead of going on shopping sprees, looking forward to prom, and hanging out with friends all day, I was taking care of my mother and sister. School wasn't helping me. I walked out her classroom and right out the building. There was no purpose for me to be in school. She had taken attendance, and I had been marked present for the day, and that was all that mattered.

I walked down the strip, taking my hair out of the ponytail it was in. It was early, and all the hustlers were hugging the block. I put my headphones in and blasted my music before walking past them. All they were gonna do was try to talk to me with no intentions on being with me or not even trying to give a bitch no bread. Just trying to fuck, and I wasn't up for the games. No one could convince me that they wanted me for me.

I had on some busted up 12's that I had been salvaging for the past three years, some ripped jeans, and a cropped shirt that I stole from American Apparel. I sat at the bus stop waiting for my bus to come. I pulled out my pad and began to draw. I drew whatever came to mind.

Through my headphones, I could hear louder music. I looked up to see a car cruising by. The window was completely tinted, so I couldn't see who was driving. Before I knew it, the window was being rolled down. I looked inside, and Jayce sat on the driver side. Jayce was the man every lady wanted a piece of. I couldn't believe he had stopped his car for me.

"Why your pretty ass sitting at a bus stop?" he said after turning his music down.

I didn't even know what to say back to him. It was the one chance I had to snatch his ass up or to make myself look stupid, but I didn't want to seem thirsty. I wasn't used to talking to men. I had my fair share of little boyfriends but nothing serious… no one like Jayce.

"Let me give you a ride," he offered.

I didn't know whether to take up his offer or to just wait for the bus. But it was too hot for me, and I was pretty sure he had his AC on blast. I rose out of my seat then walked over to his car. I opened the passenger door and hopped inside.

"Where too?"

"Edenwald Projects," I said, looking out the window and avoiding eye contact.

Edenwald was the worst place a person could live. Our projects weren't like any other projects. You weren't even safe in your house there. He put the music back up and drove as I stared out the window.

He stopped in front of a house and hopped out the truck. "I need to pick something up real quick. You can sit in the living room if you want," he said.

I shook my head. "I'll just wait here for you," I said while sitting back into my seat.

He shrugged his shoulders and walked into the house. I pulled out my pad and continued drawing again. About an hour later, I was finishing my drawing and shading, and Jayce still hadn't come out. I was pissed off, especially because I didn't know where I was.

I hopped out the car and knocked at the front door. A woman opened the door and was straight grilling me.

"Where's Jayce?" I asked, getting straight to the point.

She let the door open, and I walked in. He was sitting on the couch with different clothes on playing GTA. I was really tight. I walked over to him and snatched the controller from him.

"Bitch, you bugging the fuck out. I told your ass come in. Give me my fucking controller for I beat some sense into you," Jayce said, raising his voice while standing up.

I was ready for him to try some fuck shit, so I could pull out my switchblade and leave his ass lying in here. That nigga couldn't get pussy from me if he paid me.

"Nah, nigga! You bugging! Give me some fucking cab money or drive me home. Fuck you think this is!" I yelled back.

He dug into his pocket and pulled out a stack of twenties. He threw the money at me, and I threw the controller at him. Like a fucking kid, he continued playing his game. I picked up all the money and walked out his door. This nigga was beyond wack. I couldn't understand what all the hype was about when it came to him. If a nigga didn't respect females, I couldn't understand how girls found that attractive.

I walked out the door and back to his car and grabbed my things. I put my pen and pad in my bag and when I snatched it up altogether, his glove compartment opened up, and there were a few Benji's in there. I took that for all the time I wasted with him that I could've made some money and snatched the rosary that had to be worth more money than I had ever seen in my life. This shit was definitely going to come in clutch for me. I closed it back and stuffed the money in my panties before walking away. If Jayce thought he had just played me, he had another thing coming. I definitely played his ass. I called a cab from my phone and waited three blocks down from Jayce's house. I just wanted to get home to my mother and sister. He was going to be in for a rude awakening once he saw what I'd done, but fuck it. *Who laughs last, laughs best.* My mother always said that.

Ahmad

I sat in my office as I listened to Jay explain to me how he let some bitch get away with his money and the two-hundred-thousand-dollar rosary that his mother had saved all her life just to buy him before she passed. That shit ain't make no sense to me.

"So, some bitch you ain't know just robbed you blind?" I said, passing the blunt.

Jay and I were like brothers. We came up together in these streets. There was nothing he could tell me about these streets that I didn't know. We had been at war with niggas together tons of times. He was like the brother I never had.

"Yeah! And that bitch almost made me lose GTA!" he yelled. He was heated like it just happened to him.

"Damn, bro. When this happen?" I asked.

"Like a week ago."

"You mad about the bread or the chain? 'Cause I know you ain't bitching about ten bands when we make more than that a day.

"Nigga, I'mma kill that bitch over both. It's the fact that the bitch should've never touched what wasn't hers. I could probably let the bitch live if I got my chain back," he spat. I just nodded my head as I tied a rubber band on the knot of money.

"Where you say you met her at again?" I asked curiously.

"The forty-one bus stop."

I just nodded my head. "And where were you supposed to be taking her?"

"To the fucking projects!" he yelled, even more upset, and I began to laugh.

"Nigga, you should've known not to be messing with no project bitch. Shit, you don't hear enough of me complaining about Tiana's nagging ass?"

"When I catch that bitch, she gonna pay and that's word to my mama."

I put all the money into the safe behind my wall. I took one last pull from the blunt then walked out my office. Jay followed right behind me.

"Where you going, bro?" he asked.

"I'm gonna take Tiana and Quan to watch a movie or some dumb shit. This bitch won't stop blowing up my phone," I said, shaking my head as I looked at my ringing phone.

Jay began to laugh. "I thought y'all wasn't together?"

"That's the thing. We ain't! This bitch ain't getting the picture, and today, I'mma set that ass straight. She be draining a nigga," I said while hopping into my Benz and driving off.

I blasted the radio as I drove to Tiana's house. When I got five minutes away, I dialed her number and told her to come down. There was never any parking at her building, and I wasn't going to sit in the car waiting all day. When I pulled up to her building, she was standing out front with her two-year-old son in her arms. She sat him in the back and sat in the front seat.

"Where's his car seat?" I asked.

"Come on, Ahmad. We going right to 125th. He don't need no car seat," she explained.

I wasn't having that. The boys be trying to pull me over for my skin being too dark. She had another thing coming if she thought I was going to risk any confrontation with the law over her or her nappy headed son.

"Get back there with him, and sit him in your lap."

She pouted. "Come on, Ahmad. It's not that serious," she whined.

I looked at her like she was crazy, and she was really starting to piss me off. I was doing her a favor, and she was still giving me a headache.

"You don't know how serious it is 'cause you don't got your own car, and you ain't gonna pay my ticket with your lil' McDonald's check. So you could either sit your frail ass with him or get the fuck out so I can handle my business. I don't gotta do this, 'cause frankly, you ain't my girl, and this ain't my son."

She rolled her eyes and hopped out the front seat and got in the back, slamming both my doors. I wasn't gonna put up with this shit.

"Get out," I said to her without even turning around. She had me fucked up. I wasn't out here just dogging her. I was out here being a help to her.

"You not dead ass," she said incredulously. I got out the car and opened the door for her.

"I don't owe you shit," I spat, and she sucked her teeth before hopping out with her son in her arms.

"Remember, I don't owe you shit when you tryna get some pussy," she mumbled.

I didn't pay her no mind. There was plenty of pussy a nigga could get out here. That was the least of my worries. Just as I was about to hop back in my whip, I peeped Honesty coming out the building with a younger girl.

"Yo," I called out. She didn't turn her head, but the girl she was with did, but that didn't make her stop. I got out the car and jogged to catch up to her.

"Honesty," I said, and she stopped. "You ain't hear me call you the first time?" I asked.

"My name ain't 'yo,' so you weren't calling me."

"My fault, ma. Is it okay if I call you that?" I asked, flashing her a smile. She began to smile to.

"Ahmad, what do you want? I got things to do."

"I don't wanna hold you up, so I'mma just give you my number, and you better use it, or I'mma find which apartment it is you live in and be knocking on your door every day."

She pulled out an iPhone 4 and passed it to me.

"You ain't never seen an iPhone 4? Oh, I forgot. You too rich. You can either put your number in, or gimme back my phone, so I can go on with my day," she demanded while reaching to snatch the phone back, but I held it above her head, so she couldn't.

I figured she got offended because of my facial expression, but I didn't mean nothing by it. I just didn't remember an iPhone being so damn small. I put my number in and called my phone so I'd have her number too. I passed her the phone, and she walked away. I just stared at her walking and her outfit. There was something about her that made me want her. She looked young, so I couldn't make her my girl. We could only be friends. I walked back to my car once she got out my sight. I could feel Tiana staring a hole in my neck. I just shook my head. I looked at Quan, and he looked confused as ever. I felt bad for him.

"Get in," I called out while starting my car. She sped to the car and sat in the back with her son without saying a word as I drove to the theatre. I wasn't even doing this for her. I was doing it for her kid. His father was a deadbeat, and I tried to be there for him as much as I could. I had grown up with a father, and even though we didn't speak now, I couldn't imagine what my life would've been like without him.

Tiana was doing an okay job raising her son. A woman couldn't teach a boy how to be a man, though. I knew I wouldn't be around forever, but I definitely wanted to help the young boy grow up better than what his mother was doing.

Honesty

*H*annah and I walked from the house to the supermarket. I had a few dollars left from what I got out of Jayce. I had bought four pairs of sneakers that we could share, some outfits, and paid six months' rent. Our mom was getting sicker every day, and I couldn't stand the thought of it. It wouldn't be too long before she would have to be admitted into a hospital. I really didn't know what would happen to Hannah and I if she didn't make it.

We walked around the supermarket, spending the little bit of money we had. Once we got everything, we stood in line. After getting rang up, the total came up to $63.54. That left me with a hundred dollars. I helped Hannah carry the bags home before I jetted back out the house.

I walked four blocks down and around a corner. Justin's car was right there waiting for me. I pulled my hair into a ponytail and swallowed hard. I hated doing what I had to do to get money. I walked up to the car, and the door opened up automatically. I hopped in, and he was already in the back with his pants down to his ankles, jerking himself off. I shook my head as he closed the door and just laid there.

"How you been, Honesty?" he asked while he closed his eyes and breathed out loud.

"I'm good," I said, not wanting to have a conversation with him.

Justin looked to be in his mid-fifties if I didn't know any better and preyed on young girls who didn't know any better for money. If you brought him a baby, he would surely have his way, and although he helped me out, I hated him. I kneeled down, taking his uncircumcised dick into my hand and putting it into my mouth. He moaned like I was giving the best head ever when, in reality, I knew I wasn't.

My mouth was desert dry. I just used my hand to jerk him off until he got hard enough. Once he was hard, I sat up and began to take my pants off. I lay there with my eyes closed, saying a quick prayer. I felt him put the lubricant between my legs. I peeked out my eye and saw the thirsty look on his face. I was pretty sure he was just thinking about how good it would be to know how my insides felt. But this time wasn't going to be any different from any of the other times.

He rubbed his little dick on the opening of my vagina then began to push. I began to tighten my walls. I refused to let him take my virginity. I wanted the person who took my virginity to be someone that I loved. That was something I was giving that I could never get back, and to me, that was very important.

"Ouch, Justin! That hurts!" I said, pushing him slightly off me. He looked into my face and could see the look of pain.

"Hold up, baby girl. Let me help you feel better. He laid his body across the car and kissed on the lips that were between my legs. He stuck his tongue out and put it in my pussy. He licked all over my vagina, making me feel things I never felt before. Although I hated him, that right here made me feel like I loved him. But it was a short-lived thought, and I was thankful that I didn't think with my vagina. Business was all it was. I didn't want to show him I was enjoying it. I laid there for about ten minutes before I pushed him off and sat up.

"Damn, baby. You is ripe. Gotta let go of that virginity," he said while wiping his mouth. I ignored him while using a wipe to clean in between my legs.

"I'll let go of it when I'm ready," I said, rolling my eyes.

He looked at me and just shook his head. He pulled out a wad of money and peeled off two Benjamin Franklins. I snatched the money and stuffed it in my bra.

"Well, don't come back until you done let go," he said as I hopped out the car. I stuck up my middle finger and walked away.

Once I got to the building, I looked around the block. It was nice outside, and everybody was playing the block today. There were little girls playing double dutch in front of the building and a couple niggas shooting dice on the side. Mrs. Rivera was outside on the grill selling food. The block was hot, and I didn't really want to be in. I was almost sure Hannah would enjoy being out too. I jogged up the stairs since the elevator was broken.

Once I got in the house, Hannah was lying on her stomach across the couch on her phone. I was pretty sure she was texting one of her little fast ass friends, but I didn't care.

"Han, you wanna go out? It's nice." She sat up and nodded her head.

We walked into our room, and I pulled out flare dresses and sandals for the both of us. I hopped into the shower while Hannah got dressed. Once I got out, I brushed her hair up into a tight ponytail and put mine into a bun. Before I got dressed, and we walked out, I went into my mom's room. She didn't look like she was getting better to me.

"Dear Father God, please watch over my mother, and give her the health that she needs. Me and Hannah need her. She is our rock. Please, watch over our strong lady. Give her enough strength to fight this devil on her shoulder. Amen," I said as I opened my eyes. I kissed her forehead then walked out her room and closed her door. I walked to the front door with Hannah right on my tail.

"Honesty, do you think Mommy is gonna die?" she asked.

My heart sank to the pit of my stomach. I was unsure, but I wasn't going to let her know that.

"Not any time soon, Hannah. Pretty girls live forever."

After that, we walked out the building, and before I knew it, my shoulder went crashing backward. I looked up to see that Tiana had bumped me. I knew it wasn't an accident either.

"Watch where you going," I said, turning around to look at her. She was just grilling me, and I honestly didn't give a fuck. I turned back to continue walking, and Ahmad was sitting in his car watching me. He waved over to me.

"Honesty, come here."

I walked over to his car with Hannah by my side.

"What's happening?" I asked.

I didn't know what it was that he wanted with me. This was the first time any older guy had really been checking for me, and I wasn't used to it. After meeting Jayce's corny ass, I was uninterested, but Ahmad wasn't stopping.

"Get in, and let's ride around," he offered.

"The last time I let a stranger give me a ride somewhere, it wasn't pretty," I responded as I began to walk away.

I looked back toward the building, and Tiana was right in front still grilling me. I didn't know if Ahmad was her man or whatever, but she was barking up the wrong tree. I was going to give her something to be mad about since she was mad about her man trying to talk to me. She was going to stay mad because I was going to take her man.

I walked back to the car and hopped into the passenger seat while Hannah got into the back. I winked at Tiana before he drove off. I chuckled as she stormed back into the building with steam coming out her ears.

Ahmad

I was more than happy that I ran into Honesty again. There was something about her that was so different than everyone else. I drove to Black Tap and looked in my rearview mirror. The girl she was with had to be her little sister. They resembled one another. I looked over at Honesty, and she was already staring at me.

"What's your motive?" she asked, taking me by surprise. She didn't waste any time and got straight to the point.

I understood 100 percent why she would ask that. Everyone had a motive. "I just really want to get to know you."

"Is Tiana your baby mother or your girl?" she asked right off the bat.

"No and no," I responded.

She just nodded her head as we hopped out the car and got our ticket for the valet. We walked into Black Tap, and her sister's eyes widened at the sight of their specialty milkshake.

"Honesty, I want that," she said pointing.

"Got'chu, Han. Wait 'til we get seated first," she replied.

"How long for seating?" I asked the host.

"About an hour," she replied.

I slipped her a hundred-dollar bill, and within a minute, we were being seated. Honesty just smirked at me.

We looked at our menus for about five minutes before we ordered. I looked at her sister then her. They were both equally beautiful.

"What's your name?" I asked her sister, whose face was in her phone as she texted away.

"Hannah," she replied without looking up.

I looked at Honesty, and she was just staring at me. I could tell she was feeling a nigga. I flashed her my little crooked smile, and she tried to hide her smile and roll her eyes. She was not trying to let me in where I fit. Her phone began ringing, and she declined the call.

"That's your little boyfriend?" I asked her.

"How old are you?" she asked randomly.

"Twenty-two."

"So act your age, not your shoe size," she said, smiling. I just shook my head at the corny elementary school joke.

"How about you act your age, and stop fronting like you don't know a nigga feeling you," I said as I sat forward, challenging her.

"I don't mess with liars. You say Tiana ain't your girl or baby mama, but what other reason would you have to be coming to get her and her son for? Y'all brother and sister? I don't have time to be beefing with these corny Edenwald bitches over a nigga I barely know," she stated.

The waitress came with our food, and Hannah grabbed her cotton candy shake and began to slurp it down before anything.

"How about you get to know me then. Give me a chance at least. Just cut the act. It was cute while it lasted, but a nigga ain't gonna hurt you, ma."

"Show me you not," she said.

Those words said to me that she was going to let a nigga try with her. That was all I was asking anyway. We all ate and laughed like we had known each other all our lives.

"Ahmad, you coming over to our house?" Hannah asked. I saw the way Honesty stared at her like she had a big mouth. I just shook my head.

"Nah, but y'all can come over to my house if your sister doesn't mind," I responded.

Hannah turned her head to Honesty and put her hands together. "Honesty, pleaseeeeee! I don't wanna go home. There's nothing to do there."

"Hannah, not today. Damn. Be happy you have a damn house. You so ready to run to someone you don't even know house. Someone gon' fuck around and kidnap your little ass," she replied.

"I don't know him, but you sure enough done made him your boyfriend," Hannah said, rolling her eyes and facing her food.

"We're friends," she said right before standing up. "Now excuse me. I have to use the bathroom." I nodded my head as she rose from the seat and headed to the bathroom. Two minutes later, Hannah was standing up and right behind her.

The waiter passed me the bill, and I paid it. I picked her phone up from the table and began looking through her pictures. She had pictures of herself, her sister, her friend, and a lady who appeared to be sick. I assumed it was her mother. When she reached the table, she snatched her phone and arched her brows while looking at me.

"Nosy." She put her phone into her bag.

"Y'all ready to go?" I asked.

"Yeah. We out," Honesty responded.

We walked out and back into the car. "Should I drop y'all off back home?"

Honesty shook her head. "Drop me off on 233rd and White Plains Road."

I put my music up, and the sound of A Boogie could be heard a mile away.

"Had a knife in my back when I wrote this shit. I look back, and I laughed when I noticed it," Honesty sang along.

I turned my head to face her, and she was so into the music she didn't even notice how hard I was watching. I turned my attention to the road as the car behind me began honking. She pulled out her phone and began taking pictures with her sister. I made a mental note to myself to upgrade her phone. Once we pulled up to 233rd and White Plains, she looked out the window like she was hesitant before reaching her hand on the handle.

"Wait," I said to her as she put her hand back on her lap then looked at me. I hopped out the car and jogged over to the other side and opened the door for her. She giggled before shaking her head from side to side.

"You're such a cornball," she said as I closed the door back.

"It don't matter if you think I'm being a cornball. Chivalry isn't dead, and my mother taught me better than that," I said while looking into her eyes. We both began to get lost in each other's gaze, so she turned her face to look away. I took my hand and lifted her chin near me and brought my face to hers. I gave her a quick peck on the lips before leaning my forehead to hers.

"I ain't like these other niggas. I got you." She took a deep breath and leaned in to kiss me again, but before her lips could touch mine, Hannah was knocking on the window.

"Did y'all forget about me?" I heard her yell through the door. We both chuckled to ourselves and pulled away from each other. I opened the door for Hannah, and she held a grin on her face.

"What's so funny, punk?" Honesty asked her.

"Next time, get a room," she responded. Honesty stepped closer to me, giving me a hug.

"I'll call you when I get home," she said, pulling away. I nodded my head and hopped back into my truck before thanking God that he was convincing her to give me a chance to have her company in my life.

Honesty

$\mathcal{I}$ walked to Naomi's house, and my mind was in a completely different world. My panties were completely drenched from the kiss I shared with Ahmad. I decided I would give Ahmad a chance. That would be a first. I never gave niggas the time of the day, but Ahmad seemed a little different from the rest. He made me feel comfortable like I had nothing to worry about. Being around him made me forget about the problems in my life temporarily. I didn't want to wear my heart on my sleeve, so even though he had me right where he wanted me, I was never going to let him know that.

Once we got in front of Naomi's house, I pressed the bell, and within two minutes, she was at the door. She opened the door, letting Hannah and I inside.

"What took you so long?" she asked while walking to her room and pulling a wedgie out her ass.

"We went out to eat, and why don't you put some pants on? Nobody wanna see your black booty," Hannah responded, rolling her eyes.

"Hannah, shut up. If I wanna walk around with my vagina out, I will. This is my crib, and my momma don't have a problem seeing my black booty."

I shook my head. The two of them couldn't stop arguing with each other to save their life.

"Han, Ms. Grandberry in the kitchen," I said, directing her.

Ms. G was like a second mother to Hannah and I. Hannah bonded with her in ways she couldn't bond with my mother anymore because of her illness. They went grocery shopping together, they cooked together, and Ms. G even trusted Hannah to plant in her garden. Naomi and I couldn't even go back there unless she invited us. I was even convinced that Naomi was a little jealous of the bond between her mother and Hannah.

We stepped into Naomi's room, and I kicked off my shoes and flopped down on her bed as she on her chair at her desk, and I grabbed her iPad.

"Where y'all went to eat? And why wasn't I invited?" She pressed.

"It was a last-minute thing. And it wasn't planned. My new boo took us there," I responded as I began to blush again.

"New boo? Who? He got a friend?" she asked, sounding thirsty. We both burst out in laughter.

"Damn, Nay. Relax. I don't know if you know him, but his name Ahmad," I said. I was happy on the inside, but I was giving her a face like it wasn't all that serious.

"Ahmad? I heard that name before. In fact, if I'm not bugging, I think that's Jayce right-hand man," she said, spinning around in her chair with the Kool-Aid grin on her face.

"Jayce, Jayce?" I asked, hoping she wasn't talking about the Jayce that I had met.

"Yeah, bitch. Jayce, Jayce! The one that I'mma fuck," she said while she got up and began twerking.

"It's a small ass fucking world," I said under my breath.

"You look like I just told you I sucked Ahmad's dick. Damn, bitch. What happened?" she asked.

"The day I left school early, I was at the bus stop, and Jayce pulled up and offered to give me a ride. I took him up on his offer, not wanting to sit up in the hot ass sun."

"Damn, bitch. You fucked him before me!" she yelled. I looked at her like she was crazy.

"No, Nay! Listen, bitch! So he drives to his house, and I'm sitting in the car for like an hour. I go knock on the door, and some girl opens the door, not that I give a fuck. What baffles me is, I go in, and this nigga playing video games. Long story short, he threw four hundred at me, and I picked it up off his floor. When I went into his car to get my shit, his glove department opened. He had like three bands in there, and a rosary that had to be worth at least a hundred bands. I snatched all that shit up."

Nay had a look of worry on her face. "Damn, bitch. That's crazy. I'm guessing Ahmad don't know. Bitch, are you gonna tell him?" she asked.

I shook my head. Ahmad and I had just met, and I didn't feel the need to just come out and tell him anything. Me telling him could resort to him feeding me to the wolves, and I wasn't having that just yet.

"Sooner or later, you gonna have to come clean," she explained, and I understood, but I wasn't gonna ruin whatever this was with Ahmad over Jayce. He was an asshole anyways and deserved that shit. I was going to think of a plan and hope it worked.

Naomi and I sat there for about thirty more minutes before Hannah busted in the room.

"Dinner is ready," she said and walked back out.

Naomi and I hopped out the bed and headed straight to the dining room. On the table, there was a huge ham in a pan, some collard greens, mac and cheese, and candied yams. We pulled out our chairs and began to take a seat.

"Ew! Did y'all wash y'all hands?" Hannah asked.

"Y'all better get y'all nasty asses up and wash y'all hands. Y'all know I don't play that," Ms. G scolded.

"Snitch," Naomi said under her breath.

"Naomi, she ain't no snitch. She my extra set of eyes!" Ms. G yelled as we walked into the kitchen.

As soon as everyone was settled in their seats, we all bowed our heads as Ms. G said grace. As soon as she finished, we were passing the bowls back and forth. Eating dinner at Naomi's house was like Sunday dinner every day.

"Ma, you be throwing it down in the kitchen!" I said as I cut a piece of ham.

"I know I do, baby. Hannah is gonna know how to make everything I know how to make," she said, smiling and looking at Hannah. She nodded her head without looking up.

As soon as we were all done, Naomi and I got the dishes together and began washing. I looked at the clock, and it was pushing eight o' clock.

"Yeah, it's getting late. Let me start getting ready to go," I said to Naomi as I shot Ahmad a text to come get us. Before I knew it, he was texting me back for us to be down in five minutes.

After hugging Naomi and kissing Ms. G goodnight, Hannah and I were on our way downstairs. I recognized Ahmad's car pulling up, and we both walked over to it and hopped in.

"Y'all good?" he asked as he turned the radio down a little bit.

"Yeah. We enjoyed ourselves like we always do. What you do the whole time?" I asked.

"Play some dice games and hung with the boys. Regular shit." I nodded my head.

The thought of him and Jayce being boys crossed my mind. My stomach twisted and turned. I was feeling Ahmad, and I wasn't going to let an asshole like Jayce run him out my life. He pulled up to my building and parked his car.

"Hannah, catch the elevator," I said to get her out the car. Once she stepped out, Ahmad began to speak.

"When you gonna let me know you? The *real* you? All that you showing right now is an act. I'm not impressed," he said while looking me in my eyes and making me nervous. My gaze dropped from his, and I found myself staring at everything but him.

"I don't know what you want me to show you. You want me to let down my guard so easily, and I won't do it. I can't do it. It'll happen on its own," I replied.

He rubbed his beard before speaking again. "What are you afraid of me doing to you?"

I sat back for a minute and let his question sink in.

"I'm afraid of getting played. What a nigga like you want from a girl like me? I can't see how I'm your cup of tea if you dated someone like Tiana."

He chuckled to himself. "A nigga ain't entitled to change the tea he like? I don't play games. I'm a grown ass man. I see something in you, so I wanna pursue you." I nodded my head as I listened to what he was saying.

"Sounds good. I might be young, but you got one time to play me then I'm gone," I let him know before kissing his forehead and hopping out the car.

Ahmad

$\mathcal{I}$t had been a week since Honesty and I talked about my intentions with her. She took my word and let me in. If I wasn't out getting bread, I was somewhere with her. Even though she was young, she was old in the mind. Wasn't nothing dumb about her. I sat in my car as I waited for her to come out the building. I was about to take her and Hannah to get their hair and nails did.

With every passing day, I was realizing that I didn't want her temporarily. If she kept being real with me and herself, she definitely would be permanently mine. I watched as Tiana walked from the building and walked straight to my car.

"So this what we doing now?" she asked.

"What is you talking about now, Tiana?" I asked, looking in my rear view at nothing in particular. I just wanted her to see that I wasn't interested in talking to her.

"You walking around playing house with a preschooler? The bitch doesn't even know how to wipe her ass correctly, yet you tryna get her to suck some dick," she spat.

I was done with the conversation before it even started, and she was getting fly out the mouth.

"Watch your mouth, and what you not gonna do is walk up to me being disrespectful. You acting like we in a relationship and I cheated on you. Need I remind you that we broke up over six months ago and that you slept with my right-hand man, or did you forget?" I responded.

She was really beginning to piss me off. "Ahmad, you full of shit. You break up with me, but you and Jayce still best friends forever, right? Fuck you! I don't even know why I fucked with your corny ass," she said, walking away and flipping me the finger.

Just as she walked to the building, Honesty and Hannah were walking out. She used her shoulder to bump Honesty and turned around and smirked at me. Honesty stood in place and looked at Tiana before laughing and walking away. She and Hannah hopped into the car, and I drove off.

"She be trying me. She got one more time to bump me, and I'mma put her on her ass," Honesty said while pulling out her mirror and applying her lipstick.

She wasn't grown in age, but age was nothing but a number. As long as she didn't act like a preschooler with me. I considered her grown.

"I don't need you fighting her ratchet ass. Leave that to the bird bitches. You look too good to be fighting," I responded.

"Dead serious. A bitch like her got nothing to lose. My face too pretty to be getting bit up, scratched up, or sliced," she agreed.

"Honesty, she wasn't finna do a thing. 'Cause once you swing, I'm right over your shoulder swinging too, so she gon' have to face our wrath if she wanna fight you. Ain't no fair ones," Hannah said from the back. Honesty just nodded her head. I could see it in her face that she didn't want Hannah fighting.

About fifteen minutes later, we pulled up to the shop.

"Han, go sign our names. If they ain't got nobody, tell them you need a hot oil treatment with a deep conditioner," she told her sister.

Hannah just nodded her head and hopped out. We watched as she stepped into the hair salon before talking.

"What you doing for the day?" she asked.

"I was gonna make money moves and chill with the guys. I ain't seen them in a min," I told her as I massaged her feet that she had propped up on my lap. She threw her head back.

"That feels so good."

I began to kiss each one of her toes. They looked so perfect to me.

"Mmm," she moaned as I sucked on each one of her toes.

My hand slid up her thigh and under her dress. I stared at her with every movement, and she just lay there with her eyes closed. I rubbed her clit through her panties, and it caused her to moan again.

"Ooh, Ahmad." Her voice sounded like some sweet music to my ears. I trailed kisses up her leg, and she just rubbed my head. I was ready to get up in her right there in the car. I pulled myself back and just continued massaging her feet.

"Tomorrow, do not make any plans. It's just me and you. No Hannah… just us," she said, pulling her legs back and slipping her feet back into her sandals.

She leaned over and put her lips to mine as I grabbed the back of her head. She was looking like a snack to me. If she didn't get out, I was going to fuck her right there in the car.

"Go get your hair done while we here before I hold you hostage," I said to her. She giggled and hopped out the car.

"I'll take a cab home. I'll call you later, baby." I nodded my head and started my car and waited to see her enter the salon before driving off. It was time to make this money. Honesty had become a distraction for me. If I didn't control myself, she was going to be the death of me.

I dialed Jay's number to see where he was at and let him know what moves we were about to be making.

"Meet me at my crib," I said before hanging up.

I drove to my own home and stepped in. The smell of Honesty was on everything. I went into the refrigerator, took out some leftover takeout, and heated it up. My phone began ringing, and I thought it was Honesty, but as I looked down at it, I realized it was Tiana. I didn't even pay it any mind.

"Yoooo, bro," Jayce said as he walked in.

"What's good, bro? I ain't seen you in a minute. How everything looking at the money spots?" I asked him while sitting my food on the table and eating.

"Bro, everything on the up and up. You already know how that is. Where you been, playboy! Playing house with Tiana again?"

"Hell nah, bro. I got a new girl that's loyal and fire. But check this. She live in Tee building," I said before laughing.

"Oh shit. I'm tryna get like you. You got two hoes, one for yourself and one for the bros," he sang in a Kevin Gates like tune. I shook my head from side to side.

"It ain't even like that, bro. If anything, Tiana is for the bros," I said, thinking back to how I found her and Jayce fucking in the club bathroom when they were drunk.

"Shots fired. Nobody want her tired ass." Before I knew it, my phone was ringing again. I looked at it and saw that it was Tiana again.

"Speaking of the devil," I said under my breath while sending her to voicemail.

"Oh, you really ain't checking for her. Who your new jawn?" he asked.

"Don't worry about that. I ain't come here to talk about my girl. I came so we can talk about this money," I replied. I had learned my lesson with Tiana.

Your mans and your girl should never be close, and never discuss how good the cookie is to another nigga because they'd fuck around and try to get in the jar. That was where the feelings started come in. I was really feeling Honesty, and I doubted she'd pull the foul shit Tiana pulled, but it went both ways. I didn't want Jay to feel he could be comfortable with my girl. He had been the perfect scapegoat to get rid of Tiana's ass, but Honesty was here to stay.

"Aight, so I assigned Rich and Alpo to pick up the shipment tomorrow night at the dock. This new connect you got for us is fire. They got top of the line shit, and they shit is gonna put us at the very top," he said, getting hype.

"Yeah, Kai and Syd is my peoples from way back. Tomorrow, I'mma go collect the bread. Everybody shit should be straight."

I got up and grabbed my phone and walked to the door with Jay behind me. I locked up and hopped in my car and called Syd. Once she picked up, she didn't say a word, waiting for me to speak.

"Syd, that shipment for tomorrow… postpone it 'til next week. I got some shit to handle on my side to make sure shit go smoothly," I said while pulling out my driveway after Jay.

"Aight, Mhad. Don't make our job harder. Make it as smooth as possible. Me and Kai have retired with the gunplay and use it only if it's needed," she said.

"Got'chu, sis. One," I said, hanging up.

There was a reason for everything, and everyone didn't need to know my moves. I had a gut feeling, and my gut feeling was never wrong, but in due time, my suspicions were gonna come to light, and I knew it. I headed to pick Honesty up, so I could spend the rest of my evening with my lady.

Honesty

*A*hmad and I sat in his house watching TV while he massaged my feet. We had already dropped Hannah off with Ms. G, and we had some alone time, something we rarely had.

"My mother is sick, and there's nothing I can do to help her," I blurted out. Ahmad lifted his head up to look at me.

"You are helping her. You're taking care of Hannah the best way you know how. Her sickness is beyond your control," he spoke softly.

The tears started to form in my eyes. I knew one day I'd be waking up to no mother. "Come on, baby. Don't do this to me. You're too beautiful to be crying. Leave that to the ugly bitches," he said, trying to make me feel better while tickling the bottom of my foot.

I wiped my tears away and sat on his lap, facing him. Ahmad had really made me happy since he had entered my life. I had honestly forgotten about all my problems. I looked at him in his eyes and just wanted to show him how much I really appreciated him. I leaned in and kissed him as he ran his hand through my hair and kissed me back. He pulled away and began licking my neck. His hand went under my shirt, and I could just feel my panties getting moist. I licked his earlobe and stroked his dick from outside his pants.

He stood up and carried me into his room. He lay me on the bed and stood straight up while looking at me. I pulled off my crop top and shorts, showing him my lace Victoria's Secret thong. His dick was so hard it was pitching a tent in his pants. I could see his face, and he was about to ask me if I was sure, and I knew I was. I stood on the bed and walked over to him. I wrapped my legs around his waist and arms around his neck. He unstrapped my bra and threw it to the side and took my breast into his

38

mouth. His tongue played with my nipple as his whole mouth covered my breast. I couldn't help but moan his name.

"Ohh, Ahmad! Daddy, just fuck me," I said, wanting to get straight to the chase.

I had held on to my virginity long enough for someone I loved to take. Ahmad was the one, and I wasn't questioning it. He lay me on the bed and looked at me once more.

"You gone get it, babe. Just let me do my thing," he said before trailing his tongue from my nipple then to my navel then right to my pussy. I thought I was gonna lose my damn mind. I held his head and grinded on his face.

"Oh shit, daddy," I said as I felt an urge I couldn't control.

My legs began to shake as I tried pushing his head away, but his tongue kept moving on my clit.

"Ahmaaaad!" I screamed. I had no control over what my body was doing. After my legs stopped shaking, he kissed my lips and stood up.

"Damn, baby. Your pussy good as fuck," he said while going to reach for a condom.

As dumb as it sounded, I didn't want to use one. I wanted the full experience. I wanted to feel his skin against mine. I wanted him deep inside me.

"Put the condom away," I said, and he raised his eyebrow.

"You're my first. I wanna feel you in me," I said while stroking his dick with my feet.

He had this foot fetish that I loved. His eyes began to close. I was ready to feel his big dick inside my pussy. He climbed back into the bed and spread my legs wide open.

"If it hurt or you feel any discomfort, just tell me, so I can stop," he said.

I nodded my head and let him press his dick against my hole. As he pushed in further, I felt a pain, but I refused to tell him. It hurt but felt so good. He stroked slowly and deeply, and I was on cloud nine. Tears formed in my eyes.

"Faster, baby," I said as I felt the tingling sensation once again.

Ahmad pumped in and out of me, and all I could do was yell. It felt so good to me. Before I knew it, my legs were shaking again; I knew I was about to cum. I could feel his dick throbbing as he was getting ready to come. I squeezed my walls around his dick, and without a second thought, he pulled out and nutted all over my belly. We both lay there exhausted. After a few minutes, he got up and got me a rag, and I wiped my stomach. I hopped up out the bed and went into the bathroom to pee. I couldn't believe I had just lost my virginity. I walked back into the room, and Ahmad was still lying down but wiping his dick off.

"I really was your first," he said while looking at the little red spot on the bed.

"Duh. I wouldn't lie about that." I pulled the sheets off the bed and took it to the hamper in the bathroom.

"Linen closet is across the hall," he called out. After grabbing sheets, I fixed the bed and lay in it. All I wanted to do was be in his arms. It was one of the best nights I'd had in a long time.

While watching TV, a sadness came over me, and Ahmad sensed it.

"What's the matter, baby girl?" he asked while stroking his fingers through my hair.

"Nothing. I'm so happy you came into my life. Before, I had no way out or a way from the craziness at Edenwald, and now, you have become my escape, and I love you so much for that. With my mama dying, I don't even know how to take all this anymore. They gonna try and separate Hannah and I. With all this going on, I haven't been to school. I know there's only so much longer I can miss school before they call the people on us. I just wanna get away from everyone everywhere. I wanna leave the Bronx. This ain't nowhere that Hannah needs to be. I wanna take her upstate or something. I'mma make it happen 'cause too much be going on out here," I said in one breath.

Before I knew it, my phone was ringing. It was Ms. G. I picked it up and put it on speaker.

"Honesty," Hannah said. I could tell from her voice that something was completely wrong, like she was holding back tears.

"What's wrong, baby?" I said while getting up and finding my things.

"Mama's gone," she said. "Ms. G and I went to the house to bring her some food and she wasn't breathing, Honesty." Once those words came out her mouth, I just stood frozen.

A million thoughts ran through my head. I knew my mama was sick. I knew her life was coming to an end, but no matter how much I prepared myself for this day, the fact that reality hit was killing me. I didn't want to cry. I knew she was in a much better place. I felt bad. I just wanted to spend her last days and hours with her. I never expected for it to happen like this. Ahmad was speaking in the background, but nothing was registering. I was consumed in my own thoughts. I really had to plan the next steps for Hannah and I.

Ahmad

*H*onesty sat with the phone to her ears and tears falling down her face shook, and I could hear Hannah on the line crying. I took the phone from her and pulled her body onto mine to let her cry. I didn't know what else to do. I just knew that when my mama had died, crying was all I wanted to do, and I had nobody to hold me through it. I couldn't let my boys see me cry because I didn't want to seem weak.

I wanted Honesty to know she could let me in, and she did. She cried into my chest like a newborn baby, and I just ran my fingers through her hair. I felt bad for her. She was just talking about her moms and then received a phone call that she was dead. That was some crazy shit. Seeing her cry tugged at my heart. She was really my shorty, and her hurting was the last thing I wanted to see. I never wanted her to have a day where she was sad or miserable. She had been through so much, and I felt like God had made us cross paths because I could help her. I could help her with everything, except this part right here.

She cried until she fell asleep, and I ran my hand over my head. There was no way the system was going to get to her, but I wasn't 100 percent sure I was ready to live with a woman. It didn't even matter if I was prepared or not. She trusted me, and I gave her my word I wouldn't play her. She was my responsibility. I kissed her forehead, and she just held on to me for dear life as if I would disappear if she let go.

My phone started to ring, and I answered without checking who it was.

"Oh, you don't know how to answer my phone calls no more? You too good for me now? I know you laid up with that bitch! I hope her little hot ass give you AIDS!" Tiana barked through the phone, and I just hung up in her ear. Honesty grabbed the phone from me and blocked her number.

"I can't deal with her right now. I don't have the energy in me," she said in a raspy voice. She hopped up and put some clothes on, and I began getting dressed as well. "I need to be with Hannah," she said with her voice cracking and tears falling out her eyes.

I grabbed my keys, and we headed out the door. I drove to her friend's house, and she kissed me before hopping out. My phone began ringing from a blocked number, and I knew it was Tiana. This shit wasn't going to end with her. She wanted something from a nigga that a nigga couldn't give.

Her and Honesty were two completely different people. Honesty did what she had to do to survive, and Tiana did what she wanted to do because she could. The two were like night and day; one grew up on survival mode, and the other grew up spoiled off government assistance because she didn't want to work.

I felt bad for her son Quan. I helped as much as I could with him and wanted to continue to be around him if she allowed me, but I wanted no ties to her. Tiana could let me help her with her son or use him as a pawn to get to me. It wasn't hurting me in the end anyway. She wouldn't find any nigga who was willing to do what I wanted to do for her son. But ultimately, the ball was in her court. Her son's future depended on if she could understand that there was no us. Me and her together didn't exist. It hadn't existed in a long time, and I wanted her to stop forcing it. I decided to deal with her later, because I had something much more important on my hands to deal with.

I knew Honesty couldn't afford a funeral, so I had made my mind up that I would pay for it all anonymously. I knew Honesty well enough to know that she wouldn't allow me to spend that much money on her. Although she had let me in, she was still guarded. She was fearful of being let down, and I was doing everything to prove to her little ass that I wasn't going to fold. Actions spoke louder than words, and I respected that she thought like that.

I looked at the time, and it was 11:45 p.m. The shipment was supposed to be in at midnight. At least, that was what Rich and Alpo thought. I drove toward the docks, to a hideout that I had set up in a penthouse suite.

Whenever I wasn't with Honesty, it was time to make money. She had told me her dreams and aspirations, and I wanted to give it all to her.

I got to the penthouse, and shit just wasn't sitting right with me. Jayce couldn't smell a rat from a mile away, but I could. My senses were on point like a cat. I didn't want my suspicions to be true because then, niggas was gonna have to pay, but I needed to know what had Alpo and Rich so on edge. When the clock struck midnight, I would know for sure.

I watched as the dummy boat drove toward the dock where the shipment was supposed to take place. Anticipation was at an all-time high. This shit wasn't sitting right with me. I watched as they both paced back and forth, looking around like they weren't trying to get caught, but the pacing alone gave it away. They were making themselves hot. As soon as the clock struck midnight, the dummy boat pulled up to the dock. Just like I thought, a swarm of cop cars came through blaring. Like fire, my eyes began to blaze. I was happy I caught the shit beforehand because that would have been a whole lot of product we'd be losing.

I punched the wall out of anger because Alpo and Rich had been down for a while. There wasn't no telling how much they'd told the FEDS already. Whatever they had told the FEDS would be the last of what they told them because it was time for them to go. I dialed Jayce's number to put him on to game. It was hot, and the only people who would handle shipments going forward would be me and him. I was going to have to call Syd and Kai and let them know we were going to have to switch it up a bit.

The FEDS would faithfully wait for a shipment. Our next move had to be undetected. Jayce and I really had to go to work, because all the traps were getting shut down until we knew how to handle this situation. One thing I always said was I'd be six feet under before I took a bid. I wasn't ready to be six feet under, so it was time to switch it up, so I didn't have to be. If need be, I was going out guns blazing.

Honesty

It had been a week since my mother's passing, and I couldn't gather the correct thoughts or words to express how I felt. Hannah and I had been staying at Naomi's house. Ms. G had us bring the little bit of clothing we had over to her house. She didn't mind us staying there and took care of everything as far as my mother's funeral went. I was only eighteen. I knew absolutely nothing about how to plan a funeral. She had gone to the church and let them know of the situation, and God came through.

Someone had donated thirty thousand dollars toward the funeral and donated twenty thousand dollars to Hannah and I. When I had gotten the news, I cried like a baby. It was too good to be true. It was like God had sent me a guardian angel. I had let Ms. G hold the money for Hannah and I. It was money that we'd fall back on if anything happened.

I knocked on Ms. G's door before I walked in. Hannah sat between her legs as she did her hair. It was the last time we'd see our mother, and she had done everything to make sure we looked the part. Hannah had a black dress, and the bottom half was a long tutu. Ms. G had pulled her hair straight back into a ponytail with a big puff. She looked like the fourteen-year-old daughter my mother had left behind.

"You look nice," Ms. G said while looking at me through a mirror, and I flashed a small smile.

I had on a black long-sleeved turtleneck and a black pencil skirt with some short heels, and my hair was pulled into a top-not bun. I was ready to see my mama and also ready to get this day over with. There was no way things would get easier for Hannah and I. When shit went bad, it went bad quick. Ms. G rose from the bed and Hannah stood as well.

We walked out her room, and Naomi was sitting on the couch with a black blazer and dress pants on.

"Let's get this show on the road," Ms. G said, and we all filed out the house.

The whole ride to the church, my stomach was in knots, twisting and turning. I didn't know what to expect. I had never been to a funeral, and I never in a million years thought that the first funeral I would have ever been going to would be my mother's. I always figured it would be a friend's funeral with how ruthless these streets were, but I was wrong. I thought about Ahmad the whole ride. I hadn't seen him since I left his house, and I wanted a little bit of space.

He kept telling me he and Tiana was nothing, but she wasn't moving like it was nothing. She was moving like a bitch whose nigga was cheating on her. I didn't have the energy for it. I had bigger things to worry about, and Tiana wasn't one of them. Although I hadn't seen him, we texted every day. He checked up on me, making sure Hannah and I were straight, and I was grateful for that. I had put it in my mental to speak with him about Tiana, and it was going to be me or her. I wasn't giving her ass no more chances, so he would have to check her before I did. That bitch kept poking at the bear like a beast wouldn't come out.

The car finally came to a stop, and I took a breath while stepping out. I grabbed Hannah's hand, and we walked in with Naomi and Ms. G behind us. When we got inside, tears filled my eyes. The church was beautiful. There were pink and white roses everywhere. The pews were full of people. Ms. G had handled everything. The same way Naomi and I were best friends, there was a time where our mothers were inseparable. But like most friendships, their's ended over a man. My mother nor Ms. G never went into detail about why they fell out, and they never bashed on another. They welcomed the friendship between Naomi and I.

Everyone in the pews stood up one by one and hugged Ms. G, Hannah, and I. The loss of my mother did something to Ms. G. She didn't know it, but every night, I could hear her sniffles, and her sniffles made me begin to cry. I knew she regretted that my mother and her hadn't spoken in fourteen years over something so foolish, but my mother was gone. We took a seat in the front row and let the pastor talk. When it was time to say our final goodbyes, Hannah walked in front of me to the casket. The tears and sound of pain that erupted from her was enough to make a grown man cry. She held onto the casket for support to stand up.

"Mommy, come back!" she wailed, and everyone looked at her with sympathy in their eyes. Her cries even caused people like myself to cry even harder.

It was so hard to watch. Ms. G helped her up and walked her back to our seat. I looked down at my mother and just shook my head. My mother had fought a good fight.

"You're free now, Mama," I said as my voice cracked.

She had been fighting this demon, and she was finally at peace. I missed her dearly, but I was so happy that she was no longer in pain. I knew if my mother had to choose between an easy death or the pain that she would have to live with being alive, she'd choose living in pain because that meant being with Hannah and I. I was okay with her being gone, but that didn't make the pain any better. I just knew that she had prepared me and raised me well enough to know how to handle myself. And despite her and Ms. G's differences, she knew she'd left us in good hands.

I took a final look at her and noticed that she no longer looked sick, she looked like her old self, the mother I remembered. I was happy that Ms. G had handled everything accordingly. Even the casket was beautiful. She had really outdone herself. I kissed her lips, and a teardrop fell from my eye onto her cheek. It looked as if the tear had come from her own eyes.

"I love you, Ma, and I'mma take care of Hannah the best way I know how," I whispered before walking away and taking a seat beside Hannah.

I grabbed her hand and squeezed it. I wanted to assure her that we were going to be okay. We always ended up okay in the end.

When the funeral ended, everyone headed back to my mother's house. Ms. G had catered soul food from Manna's, and everyone enjoyed themselves and mingled. I walked into my mother's room, and Hannah sat on her knees at the bedside crying. I didn't know how to make her feel better. There was no amount of words that I could say that could make the pain go away. The same pain she felt tugged at my heart as well. I sat beside her and squeezed her into a hug until she stopped crying. When the tears wouldn't come anymore, I grabbed her hand and led her into the kitchen.

Just as I was about to make her a plate, I received a text message from Ahmad.

Ahmad: *Come downstairs*

I turned to Hannah and passed her the plate.

"I'll be right back, Han. Please, eat," I begged, and she nodded her head.

I walked out the building, and Ahmad standing outside of his car with a bouquet of pink and white roses. I gave him a small smile, as it was all I was able to give. I began to walk toward him when Tianna bumped against my shoulder roughly, causing me to take two steps back and almost knocking me on my ass.

I reached for my pocket, realizing I didn't have my switchblade. I punched her straight in the nose. She had this ass whopping coming, and deep down inside, I was happy she decided to try me. I had so much pent up anger in me that needed to be released, and she had just set herself up. She swung on me and grazed my face, and I grabbed her long weave, pulling down on it, causing her to lean down to my side. I punched her face, and the force of it spun her around until she hit the ground. Once we were on the ground, I was on top of her ass, sending blows to her face. I didn't care for punching her body. I wanted to fuck her face up. So every time she looked in the mirror, she had a reminder to stop fucking with me. I felt Ahmad tugging at me, but I wasn't letting up. He pulled me off of her, but my hand stayed in her hair. She was going to have a bald spot if he didn't let go, and he didn't. I kept pulling and kicking at her face until I drew blood. It trickled down her face, and I continued kicking her.

"I keep letting you slide, bitch, but you keep fucking trying me!" I yelled while trying to continue punching.

"Honesty, chill out!" Ahmad said, raising his voice at me, but I didn't care about that. It wasn't the day. She kept trying me and trying me, so she was getting what she wanted.

Bystanders tried to get me to release her hair. I yanked hard one last time, and the track came out, and she fell on her ass. Ahmad put me in the back seat of his car before getting in the driver's seat. and driving off before the police came. He wasn't gonna hear the end of this shit neither.

"You're the reason this bitch keeps playing with me! Before you were checking for me, ain't nobody around here bothered me! You came to me!

You shouldn't fucking have if you knew what the fuck what going on between y'all wasn't over!" I yelled, getting upset all over again.

The tears began to fall from my eyes. I wanted to fight his ass too, but I didn't have the energy in me.

"Take me back to my fucking mother house! The next time that bitch try me, I'mma bury her and that fucking baby!" I spat.

Ahmad said nothing. He let me rant and rave until he got back to in front of my building. Tiana was sitting on the corner, trying to get herself together. I hopped out the car and headed straight back upstairs. I didn't have time for the bullshit. I didn't come downstairs for that. I hadn't seen him all week, and I missed him so much, but he had me fucked up. I wasn't going to play the games he played. I was living fine without him, and I knew I could resume living without him. I didn't want to, but I would if I had to. I wasn't going to allow Ahmad, or anyone else for that matter, to bring stress to my life.

When I got back into the house, Naomi noticed the scowl on my face and followed me to the bathroom. I looked in my mirror, and I looked untouched. You couldn't even tell I just had to beat a bitch's ass.

"Wassup?" she asked, standing behind me while I fixed my bun.

"I just had to beat Tiana's ass. That hoe been trying me since Ahmad been wanting me. I been letting her slide, but now, the bitch downstairs with her face leaking," I said with a shoulder shrug.

Naomi chuckled and shook her head. "That broad should've just leave you be. They don't know that when Honesty ain't bothering someone to leave her the hell alone?" she asked half-jokingly.

"They don't know, Nay," I replied.

I had always been a fighter from grade school to high school. I had recently learned to control my anger, and like I said, Tiana had earned that ass whopping. I shook my head and walked out the bathroom with Naomi behind me. I went to the kitchen, and we both made ourselves a plate and took a seat beside Hannah. It hadn't hit me that this was our last time in this apartment. This apartment was all we knew. Everyone from the block knew us, and it was bittersweet. This block held all our memories. I ate, and tears began falling from my eyes. Hannah and I were motherless children.

Ahmad

Three weeks had gone by since Honesty went off on me. I wasn't going to front. I was missing my lady. Her little eighteen-year-old ass had me acting in ways that nobody ever had me. I was blowing up her phone, but of course, I didn't get an answer. I knew better and wasn't giving up. I had given her the space that I felt like she needed, but a nigga's heart was yearning for her. I was trapping day and night to keep my mind off her. I had sent flowers with notes, chocolates, them little edible fruits that females like, and I still wasn't getting an answer.

I rolled up a blunt and let the weed take over my mind. I sent her a text and waited for it to say delivered, and it never did. I frowned. I put the blunt down while getting up and grabbing my car keys.

I pulled up to her friend Naomi's house and I spotted her walking down the street. I knew that walk anywhere. She had on shorts that her ass hung out of, a cropped t-shirt, her hair in a messy bun, and some Nike slides on. I put the car in park and jogged down to her. She didn't even know that I was watching her. She went into the store on the corner, and I walked in right behind her. Just as she was about to order food, I stepped in front of her

"You blocked my number?" I said, getting straight to the chase.

She knew a nigga was feeling her, but she wasn't gonna play me like no wack ass nigga. There were multiple bitches who were in line to fuck with a nigga, but my eyes were only on her. I just needed clarification on what we were doing, so she could stop with the cat and mouse games.

"I didn't block shit. My phone broke. What? You stalking me now?" she said while rolling her eyes.

I was unfazed by it all. I grabbed her hand and walked out the store with her behind me.

"Ahmad, stop pulling on me," she whined as we got to the car.

"Get in," I said in a serious tone.

She got in without saying another word. I hopped in and began driving to the Apple store.

"Where you are taking me?" she asked, and I ignored her question and asked one of my own.

"Why you got on these short ass shorts?"

"It's only 101 degrees out. What should I have on? A sweat suit?" she replied sarcastically.

"Make me no never mind what you got on. Just don't have one of these little niggas out here getting fucked up," I retorted while turning the radio on.

She sat back and stopped talking, but a small smile crept up on her lips. That smile was breathtaking. It felt like I hadn't seen her smile in ages. She put her hand on my lap and massaged my dick through my pants.

"Keep playing, ma. A nigga gon' fuck around and crash this shit," I said once I felt my dick jump. That nigga had a mind of his own.

"Then you should keep your eyes on the road, and make sure we don't crash," she replied while pulling my john out my pants.

Before I could say something back to her, I felt her warm mouth wrap around the head as she bobbed down, letting it hit the back of her throat. She went fast then slow, making me drive faster and slower. Her hands massaged my balls.

"I'm 'bout to nut," I said while driving through a red light.

She began going faster, and before I knew it, red, white, and blue lights were flashing behind me. I slowed down, and just as the car stopped, I exploded in her mouth. She sat up and swallowed my kids and looked me in the eyes with a smile. The officer tapped my window, and I shook my head at her.

"You fucking crazy," I said while fixing myself and rolling down the windows. This was a ticket I wasn't even going to try to talk myself out of.

"Excuse me, sir. License and registration. Do you know why I pulled you over?" the officer said, giving his spiel. I gave him a blank stare while passing him my shit.

"You gon' tell me why, aren't you?" I said, cutting straight to the chase.

"You were going sixty in a forty, and you ran three red lights. I'll be right back," he said while walking away.

Them pigs were going do what they wanted to do, and I wasn't going to entertain them. I was ready for the nigga to give me my ticket, so I could go on with my day.

I turned to Honesty, and she had one leg up on the dashboard and was playing in her pussy. I had no idea what the fuck had gotten into her, but this wasn't the same person that had lost her virginity a few weeks ago. Either she'd been fucking another nigga, or she was watching too much porn.

I looked in the rearview mirror and saw that the officer was still in his car, so I focused back on her. She was moaning and staring me in my eyes. Her fingers were drenched in juices, and all I wanted to do was taste. Something told me the minute I dived in between her legs, that would give the officer a reason to pull out his gun, and I wasn't going to risk it. I moved her hands and began playing in it and watching the juices come out as she licked her fingers.

"I'm cumming, daddy! Oh my God!" she squealed as she came all over my leather seats.

I looked back in the rearview, and the officer was no longer in his car. Instead, he was right by my window. He cleared his throat, and his white ass face was bright pink.

"You're good to go," he said with his voice shaky, I snatched my shit out his hand and sped off.

I turned to Honesty, and she was getting herself cleaned up. She wasn't getting away with that, that easily.

"Where the hell you learned to do all that?" I asked with a raised eyebrow, and she laughed loudly.

"I ain't got no dick in almost a month. Porn and these fingers have been my best friend," she said, blushing.

I shook my head. I knew something had to give. She began flipping through the radio stations, and I drove while admiring her.

"You missed a nigga, huh?" I asked.

"Ehhh, just a tad," She replied while putting her fingers up with a small space in between. She had no idea how much a nigga missed her.

We pulled up to the Apple store, and I hopped out and went around to her side and opened the door. She hopped out, and her ass jiggled, and I couldn't help myself but to pin her against the car. I put my hand in her hair and fisted it while pulling her closer her to me and sticking my tongue down her throat. I wanted to swallow her whole because she was just that beautiful. A nigga couldn't deny it. After about five minutes and various people walking around staring, I pulled away and put my hand around her waist, leading her into the Apple store. Her face lit up like a baby in a candy store, and I just chuckled and shook my head.

"Go talk to one of the people who work here and get whatever phone you want. I'mma be over here at the laptops," I said while looking at her ass through the shorts. I wanted to stick my face all up in there at that moment. She had no idea.

Her eyes widened at me, and she began jumping up and down like a kid, which caused us both to laugh.

"Go 'head, ma," I said, shooing her away while walking over to the table of MacBooks.

I sat at the computer and began searching for event planners. Honesty didn't know, but I remembered that her birthday was the upcoming weekend. She wasn't going to have a clue what the plan was, and that was exactly what I wanted. Women loved surprises, even the ones who didn't. It wasn't the surprise itself that made them shocked; it was the fact that someone had thought of them and went to great lengths to do something that wasn't expected.

No matter how hard Honesty tried to front, she wasn't going nowhere. I knew the way a nigga's heart was hurting that her's was too. My own mama didn't make my heart feel the way it felt when I hadn't spoken to Honesty in two weeks, and that was how a nigga knew she was it. A nigga was ready to settle down with her and only her. The age difference didn't matter. The chemistry and history is what did, and for the two of us, it was undeniable.

Honesty

onique's salon chair was beginning to get uncomfortable while she curled my hair, and her makeup artist did my face. It was my birthday, and Ahmad wanted to take me out somewhere special. He planned my entire day out. I had been getting pampered from the minute I woke up. He had taken me to get my nails and feet done, and since it was my birthday, I figured "why not go all out?" I got my nails done in a long, stiletto shape and junked up with rhinestones. Nobody couldn't tell me nothing. This was the most anyone had gone all out for me. The fact that I had no spending limit was what excited me. I had gone from someone who had nothing to someone who wasn't without anything. I looked at the time, and it was pushing 10:30 p.m., and he was supposed to be picking me up at 11:00p.m.

"Y'all almost done?" I asked anxiously. I felt like I'd been sitting in the chair for over three hours. My patience had definitely run thin.

"Perfection takes time, boo. If you walking around saying we did it, you gotta walk out here looking like Queen Bey, not Hazel E," Monique said as she swooped a bang across my face. She ran her fingers through my hair to loosen it up a bit, and then a wide smile crept up on her face.

"You walking out here like the queen bitch. Don't ever rush me," she said while spinning my chair to face the mirror.

My breath got caught in my throat when I laid eyes on myself. I never thought I could be so beautiful. From the glitter on my eyes to the mocha-colored lip gloss I had on my lips, I looked perfect like a Barbie doll or *America's Next Top Model.*

My eyes began to water up, but I wasn't about to fuck my face up. I threw my head back, forcing the tears to go back to where they came from.

"Bitch, cry if you want. I slayed your shit. It's waterproof," the makeup artist said confidently while giving a smile.

A car horn began to blow, and I knew it was for me. "How much I owe you?" I asked while digging in my pocketbook.

"Girl, bye. Ahmad already handled it all," Monique said as she grabbed the broom and began sweeping.

I pulled out two fifty-dollar bills and set them on the counter before walking out. When I walked out, the limo that Ahmad had me riding in all day was sitting out front. The driver came out and opened the door for me. When I stepped inside, I was surprised by white roses sitting on the seat, a Kay Jeweler's bag, and a Dare to Be Vintage Shane Justin bag. Like a kid in a candy store, my eyes beamed. I was forever grateful for Ahmad. He had shown me how a man should treat a lady, and I knew to never take anything less than the best. I had let my guard down when it came to him. I feared where we were going with this relationship, but he made me feel good and like a woman, and nobody had treated me as such.

I looked in the jewelry bag and pulled out two boxes. I opened the first one, and inside, was a princess-cut diamond studded necklace. My jaw literally dropped to my chest. Inside the smaller box was the matching bracelet, and at that point, I couldn't help it but to shed a few tears. They weren't tears of sadness but tears of happiness. I hadn't been this happy ever in my life. I looked in the Dare to be Vintage bag and pulled out a Ferrari-red dress. I pulled it to my chest and lay back onto the seat. He had really outdone himself at that point. He made me feel like a princess, and there was no denying it.

When the limo came to a stop in front of Ahmad's house, he came out and opened the door. I couldn't help it but to jump on him, wrapping my legs around his waist and kissing him like it was the last kiss I'd get.

"Get dressed, ma. We already behind schedule," he said while putting me down on my feet.

I rushed into the house and took a bird bath while trying not to mess up my hair and makeup. I slipped on the dress, and just like I thought, it fit like a glove. He came up behind me, putting on the necklace he'd bought me, and I put on the bracelet. I opened the box on the bed, and it was as if every surprised bone had left my body. I opened the Christian Louboutin box, and an exclusive pair of red bottoms were sitting inside. I just shook my head and slid them onto my feet while grabbing a clutch. Ahmad stood back and licked his lips while looking at me, and I licked my lips looking at him too. He looked like he was trying to get fucked rather than go out. He had on a suede blazer and matching pants that were the same shade of red as my dress, and his black loafers stood out.

"You know we ain't gotta go nowhere, right? I'm ready to fuck you all up and down this house," I said jokingly, looking him dead in his eyes.

"Go on with that shit, and let's go." He chuckled while flashing that million-dollar smile.

I grabbed his hand, and we walked to the limo. The minute we got inside, I was all over him. He pushed me down onto the seat and pulled my dress up while sliding my thong to the side. He flicked his tongue on my pearl, and I jumped up at the touch. The way he made me feel was almost sinful.

He dove in face first and licked on my peach like it was his last meal. I was so wet that not even all the slurping he did could stop me from wetting the seat. I ran my fingers through his hair and grinded my hips on his face.

"Ohh… baby… yess. Right there," I said in between moans. I felt myself about to climax, and he pulled back, inserting his fingers in me.

The driver turned the music up louder to drown out the moans, but I didn't care. This was a feeling that was heaven sent. He used his tongue and flickered across my clit a few times, and there it was—my first birthday orgasm.

Ahmad pulled away and grabbed a wipe and passed it to me. I wiped in between my legs and fixed myself. Before I knew it, the car was stopping. I looked in the mirror to make sure that everything was still on point. After applying on some more lip gloss, I stepped outside of the car. We were at Webster Hall, one of the ille st clubs in the city. There was a line going down the street for entry. As we walked through the doors, there was no music playing, and all the lights were off. I was confused for a second, but then the light flashed and all I heard was "Surprise!" My mouth fell open in shock. The first person I spotted was Naomi, and she laughed and took a picture of my expression.

I turned to Ahmad and clung onto him as the tears fell from my eyes. He had thought my entire birthday through when, in reality, he didn't have to do all this. He made me feel a way about life that I hadn't felt before. I was genuinely happy, and it was all thanks to him. The glitz the glam was all new to me, and I loved him for it all. I pulled away from him, and the lights dimmed, and the music began blaring.

"Come on, ma. Tonight's all about you. Let's enjoy the night," he said while pulling me toward a section.

Naomi had already started popping bottles. I was sipping and enjoying myself. Even Ahmad seemed relaxed, and I figured it was because it was his own event, and he had shit on lock.

"Come on, girl. Let's go dance!" Nay said while pulling my hand and dragging me to the dance floor.

It was as if the DJ knew we were young and ratchet he played "Twerk" by City Girls and Cardi B. Naomi and I began twerking our asses off. I twerked so much I had to hold the bottom of my dress down in order to stop it from rising. Naomi was free to twerk however she liked in the romper she had on. As the other girls in the club twerked, Naomi stole the spotlight, and I stopped and began throwing bills at her. This was a proud best friend moment.

As I began throwing bills, other dudes began throwing bills at her too. This only gassed up her ego, causing her to get on her head top and twerk. Once I saw that her pussy was peeking through the short romper shorts, I pulled her up to her feet, and she collected her money. We laughed together and walked away.

While walking, a dude about my height with a suit jacket, a cane in his hand, and gators on his feet walked up to Naomi. When he opened his mouth, he had a mouth full of gold.

"Damn, ma. What you did out there was dope as fuck? I'm Trick, and you are?" He said while flashing her a smile full of gold teeth.

"I'm Naomi. Nice to…" Before she could finish her sentence, security was escorting him out.

I looked up at our section, and Ahmad was staring down at us with a mean mug. I didn't have a clue what had just happened, but I was sure going to get to the bottom of it… just not tonight. Tonight was designed for me to enjoy myself, and that was exactly was I was doing.

We went back to our section, and about thirty minutes later, there was a two-tier, topsy-turvy princess cake coming out with sparkle candles.

"Happy birthday to you!" everyone in the section sang.

The DJ continued to sing the song over the microphone. I couldn't believe that everyone was showing me so much love. I felt like a hood princess. When I blew out my candles, the DJ put the music back on, and everybody resumed partying and bullshitting. I stood from my seat, and as I walked toward the balcony to overlook the party, I felt someone bum rush me while wrapping their hands on my neck. I turned around, and I was face to face with the devil himself. He squeezed on my throat, and I clawed at his hand while looking around for Ahmad.

"Where's my fucking chain, bitch?" Jayce spat in my ear.

Like a knight in shining armor, Ahmad hit him over the head with a pistol and yoked him over the balcony.

"Fam, don't ever put your hand on my lady ever again," he spat into his face.

For the first time in a long time, I was scared. Things could go one of two ways. They could throw down, or Ahmad could end him. At that point, everyone in our section was looking as the chaos ensued.

"You going against your brother for a bitch who stole from me!" he yelled, pushing Ahmad in his chest.

Ahmad put the gun away and had Jayce escorted out the club. Although he was gone, tension was at an all-time high. I didn't know what would happen if Ahmad found out I'd stole from his best friend, and I wasn't ready to find out. I sat down and sipped on my drink for the entire night while Ahmad sat down like he was in a trance. I had to get my shit together before the questioning started.

Ahmad

The drive back to the house was quiet as hell. The night wasn't supposed to go the way it went. With Trick popping up preying on bitches then Jayce pulling that foul shit, I didn't know what to believe. He had made accusations, but Honesty never denied it. I didn't know if it was true, or if she really just didn't give a damn what he was talking about because it was untrue. The shit that pissed me off was Jayce didn't speak to me and let me get to the bottom of it. He was out here trying to squeeze the life out my lady, and I wasn't having it.

When we pulled up to the house, there was nothing but silence. I had questions, and I was going to get the answers tonight. She walked into the bedroom and began taking off her clothing, and I went to my dresser and took off my Rolex.

"You got something to tell me?" I started while unbuttoning my shirt.

Without batting an eye, she replied nonchalantly. "No. Aside from the bullshit, thank you for everything tonight."

I walked over to her and picked her face up, so she could look me in my eye.

"How you know Jayce?" I asked, looking straight in her eyes to see if there was any nervousness, uncertainty, or fear.

"I don't. I know of him. But apparently, he thinks he know of me," she replied.

"Who was the man that stepped to Nay?" she added.

I walked away. I didn't want to get into details about Trick.

"Nobody good. She should stay away from him 'cause he'll get her in some shit she can't get herself out of," I said.

Trick was the new age pimp. He lured women in and had them

thinking they were his woman then put him on the strip to work for him. He used to be the big-time dope man back in the day but fell off when he got caught up by them pigs. His new forte was prostitution, and they couldn't pin shit on him because he had them bitches wrapped around his finger. They would do a bid for him without batting an eye. I didn't want Honesty around him, and that meant saving her friend. My job was to protect her, and I was going to do that by all means necessary, even if it meant falling out with a bro.

I had let Jayce slide when it came to Tiana because my feelings never ran that deep. But Honesty was my soft spot. She was who I'd want to mother my kid someday. She was going to get wifed up, and I didn't want nobody to feel like they could get comfortable enough to be disrespectful —Jayce included. I knew he was going to be in his feelings about the shit, but I was okay with it.

He had crossed a line, and I was cool with just being business partners. I finished undressing and followed Honesty into the shower. The minute I stepped in, she dropped down to her knees, not caring that the water was fucking her hair up and began deep throating my dick. I grabbed a fist full of her hair, and she moaned while bobbing her head back and forth. She used one of her hands to play with herself, which made my dick want to burst right there.

I picked her up off her knees and pinned her against the shower wall while sliding in and out of her. The wetness of her pussy and the sound of our bodies making music made me groan out loud. She used her tongue to lick my ears and neck, and without pulling out, I nutted in her. Her body went limp, and she slid down the bathroom wall. We stood face to face, and I washed her entire body. She was everything I needed and more.

After we showered, I picked her up, put her robe on, and lay her on the bed. I put my boxer briefs on and lay behind her. She was home for me. This was where I wanted and needed to be.

"Move in," I said while rubbing my hand through her hair.

"I can't leave Hannah," she said in a soft tone.

I stood to my feet and grabbed her hand while walking to the guest room. I had planned for this. When I opened the door, her mouth dropped open. What used to be the guest room had been renovated and made into a room for Hannah. The walls were striped with purple and pink, and a canopy bed sat in the middle of the room. While Honesty wasn't dealing with a nigga, I took some time out my day to put this together for her sister. What better moment was there to show her? She faced me with a small smile.

"You full of surprises, lil ugly ass." I chuckled and playfully mushed her head.

"So is this home or what?" I said, trying to get an answer out of her.

"This is home. This is home," she said while facing the room again.

* * *

THE NEXT MORNING, I woke up to the sound of my phone ringing. When I looked at the caller ID, it was Jayce. I looked over at Honesty, who was sleeping peacefully, and kissed her forehead before getting up and answering.

"Yo."

"Last night you pulled some foul shit over a bitch you barely know. Meet me at the crib in an hour," he replied then hung up.

I shook my head and went back to bed with Honesty. I wasn't tripping off Jayce. He wanted to meet, so we would meet. I kissed her on her neck and traveled down to her navel, and her entire body shuddered.

"Ahmad," she groaned groggily.

"Baby, you sound like a man. Just hush," I said while continuing to kiss her. She laughed and playfully hit me on the head.

When my face was directly in front of her pearl, I kissed it like it was the lips on her face. It was so soft and smooth having my face in between her legs. It felt like being on clouds. I licked, and she grabbed the sheets while wrapping her legs around my neck. Shit, if she squeezed a nigga to death, I'd die a happy one. I licked, sucked, and played until I felt her body tense up. She tried pushing my head away, but this was what I antici-pated. She let out a loud moan before cumming, and I licked it like a kid eating an ice cream cone.

Once I got done, I kissed her pussy one last time before getting up.

"I gotta meet up with Jay about what happened last night," I said while walking into the bathroom.

She said nothing. I brushed my teeth and walked back into the bedroom to get dress, and she was asleep like she hadn't even woken up in the first place.

I threw on a jogging suit and some Huarache running shoes and headed out the door. I was hoping to be back by the time she woke up, so I could take her to Ms. G's house to get her things. I put Jay Z on blast as I took my time getting to Jayce's house. I was in no rush. He was all emotional when, in reality, I had no hard feelings. I just wanted him to know there was a line that couldn't be crossed with Honesty.

After about fifteen minutes, I was pulling up to his street. I grabbed my Glock 43, putting it in my ankle. I didn't know what type of time we were meeting on. And with the way he sounded on the phone, I wasn't giving nobody no chances. I walked up to his door and knocked, and like he had been waiting on me, he opened right away. I stepped in, and he had a grill on his face that he wouldn't fix, but it wasn't moving me. I took a seat on the couch, put my hands together, and sat forward.

"Wassup? You ain't call me here for a staring contest, so speak up," I said.

"I told you that bitch stole from me, and you made her your shorty. You ain't even tell a nigga. Then you gon' try to G check me in the club? Since when we do that!" he yelled.

"Nigga, you told me you got robbed by a shorty. You never gave a name or a face. And then you yoking up my lady at a party that I threw for her? Nigga, she ain't Tiana, and as my bro, you could've came correct. You worried about what me and my lady got going on when you should be worried about them snitch ass niggas tryna set us up with the FEDS."

"Nah, nigga! You worried about the wrong things! If your head wasn't so far up the bitch's ass, you would've known that I handled that situation already! Fuck that bitch! She stole a chain my mama gave me, and you gon' bag and wife that bitch! At least Tiana ass ain't out here stealing!" he yelled louder. Spit was flying out his mouth, and the veins in his neck were protruding.

I couldn't understand why he was so worked up. I stood to my feet and went closer to him, so he could understand my next few words.

"Watch your mouth when you speak of her. She said she ain't take the chain. If it was important to you, you should've never left the shit in the car. But that's what your irresponsible ass do all the time nigga," I said calmly, but I could tell that my words bothered him because I saw his hand going down to his waistband.

"What? You gon' shoot me, nigga? Shoot me!" I said while raising my voice.

He kept his hand on his waistband and began to speak. "That chain is 150 bands. You gon' run me my money, or I'mma get it another way."

He took a step closer to me, sizing me up. Jayce didn't put an ounce of fear in my heart. His bold talk only infuriated me.

"Nigga, get it another way then," I said while turning my back to him and walking out the door. Just like that, a thirteen-year brotherhood went out the window.

Honesty

*I*t had been a week since the party, and everything was going as smooth as ever. I had told Ms. G that Hannah and I would be moving in with Ahmad, and she gave her blessings. She insisted that Hannah spend weekends with her, and that, I didn't mind. Ahmad and I needed our alone time anyways, and weekends would do. I sat on Naomi's bed with her while waiting on Ahmad to come pick us up for the last of our stuff.

"Bitch, you been getting so much dick you ain't got time for me no more." She laughed, and I laughed too because I couldn't deny it.

"Hush up, hoochie. I always got time for your mixy ass. What's news?" I asked, being nosy. I hadn't gotten any tea from her as usual, and I knew she had some piping hot tea to spill.

"Word on the street is Jayce and Tiana are an item. You're the reason Jayce and Ahmad ain't fucking with each other no more, annnnd guess what?"

I was baffled, but not really. Naomi kept her ears to the streets. Jayce and Tiana? I wondered if Ahmad knew. Would he even care? I wasn't saying shit because I felt like his ass wouldn't care about whatever the hell that bitch had going on.

"What? You got a new man?" I asked, raising my brows. From the smile that spread across her face, I could tell I hit the nail on the head.

"Yes, bitch. Remember that nigga Trick from your party? He been feeling a bitch and spoiling her," she said, overly excited.

She was grinning hard like she had won the lotto. I wasn't as enthusiastic at that point because Ahmad had warned me about him, but I had to see what she knew about her new man.

"Spoiling you? Bitch, what he doing? Selling drugs?" I asked, trying to get info out of her, but she shrugged her shoulders.

"I don't know. I only went out with him twice, and the nigga has already bought me two Gucci bags and a Chanel bag. He could sell ass for all I care. Long as he keep bringing me shit like this, I'mma be around," she said, sounding really excited like she'd made her mind already.

So I wasn't going to burst her bubble. Nay was going to do what Nay wanted, and I didn't want to seem like I was hating.

"Alright, boo. Be careful. And find out what that man do so you don't ever be caught up in no shit," I said while my phone began to ring. I knew it was Ahmad, and he was probably calling to tell me to come down. I gave her a hug and grabbed the last two bags of clothes.

"Bitch, don't be a stranger. I better see your ass and get a phone call every day," she said, and I could see her eyes glistening with tears.

"Nay, stop. I ain't dying. Just moving out."

She burst out in tears, which caused me to cry with her. I was taking a next step in my life by moving in with Ahmad, and whether she knew it or not, I was scared. We had only lived together for a short period of time, but we had been friends since forever. There wasn't a memory that I had that Naomi wasn't there for, but we were both growing up, and it wouldn't be like old days where we could just sit in each other's faces, not doing anything. We had our own lives to live, and I was happy but nervous and scared all at the same time.

"Bitch, Sundays are for us. How about it?" I suggested.

I always had Naomi as a listening ear, and I needed her around. She was a part of me; she witnessed my glow up. I gave her one last hug and hauled the bags to the door, and the minute I opened it, Ahmad was right there.

"Can you take these down? I wanna go talk to Ms. G."

He nodded his head, and I turned back to walk into the house. I knocked on her bedroom door, which was slightly open, and pushed it open a little more. She was there hugging Hannah and rocking back and forth.

"I'll see you Friday, love bug," she said while kissing her on the forehead.

"Hannah, the car is downstairs," I said as I walked up to Ms. G. She walked out the room, leaving the two of us together.

"Ms. G, thank you for everything. I can't even express how thankful I am for you, and if my mother was here, she'd thank you to the moon and back."

"Not before cursing me out," she replied with a small chuckle. Tears began to form in her eyes. We had never spoke on my mother. "Man, I wish I could just tell her sorry and gain back all the years we lost together. Honesty, don't ever let anything get in between you and your sisters," she said while taking a sigh.

I didn't know if she was talking in circles or trying to let me know something. I had spoken of Nay like she was my sister, but this was the first time Ms. G had said it. It was something about the way that she said it that made me want to ask questions.

"What did happen between you and Mommy, Ms. G? I remember y'all being the best of friends, then around the time Hannah was born, everything changed."

She took a seat on her bed and patted beside her for me to take a seat.

"Your mother and I used to be inseparable. When she first had you, I made a mistake of sleeping with your dad. She forgave me for that, even though I was pregnant with his child. She said no man could ever come between us, and she got rid of him for the sake of the both of us, and he disappeared." My mouth dropped open, and before I could even ask questions, she nodded her head. "You and Naomi are kin," she added while tears fell. "Even after having Naomi, your mother still trusted me. Our relationship remained the same in every aspect, except when it came to men. We avoided speaking of men, neither of us wanted to bring up the past, and it worked. She had found a man, and so did I, but because of the past, we never got into detail. Your mother was in love with this man. She even got secretly married to him and didn't tell me. But who could I blame? I messed up that relationship we had.

Your mother got pregnant with Hannah, and the day she gave birth, I went to visit her, and her husband was there. I was the one to tell her for a second time we shared another man. There was nothing I could say to her to make her believe that I didn't know he was her husband, but it was true. I had no clue. Revealing the truth this time, it was different, though. We spoke only about you girls, and she never forgave me. We had always vowed that whatever happened between the two of us had nothing to do with you and your sisters. I didn't know that they were married. When I told her the truth, she never looked at me the same." She wept.

I didn't know what to do as she cried onto my shoulder. I felt bad. My mother was gone, and there was nothing I could do. I didn't hold a grudge against her, although I could have. If she would've never slept with my dad or Hannah's, our life probably could have been different, but it wasn't, and I couldn't fault her for it.

My life had gotten better. After finding out Nay and I were sisters, I didn't know how to feel. A million questions ran through my mind. Did she know all this time? Was she hiding the truth from me? As if she could read my mind, she began speaking again.

"You know Nay can't hold water, so no, she doesn't know any of this. I would like to keep it that way. I just want you girls to remain how you've always been. I never want history to repeat itself. When I see you two together, I see your mother and me, and it brings me joy."

"I won't say a thing. You've done so much for me and Hannah. Let's just say my debt is paid," I said while standing up and giving her a big hug. "I love you, Ms. G. Forever and always."

"I love you too, baby. Don't forget to bring Hannah on Fridays, please. I need her just as much as she needs me." I nodded my head before walking out her room and out the door.

Once we got to the house, Ahmad brought all our things in before heading back toward the door.

"I'mma go handle some business at the trap. I'll be back."

"Bring back some pizza, please. I'm starving," Hannah said as she opened up the fully stocked refrigerator.

With all that cooking Ms. G had taught her, she'd rather pizza than a home-cooked meal. I shook my head as I began hauling the bags into the bedrooms.

"Got you, lil' boss," he replied with the nickname he'd made up for her before walking out the door.

As I unpacked my things, the chain I had jacked Jayce for fell out and onto the floor. My heart skipped a beat. Ahmad wasn't home, but just the mere thought of him finding out about the chain had me shook. I had never really lied to him before, and I didn't know how he'd react finding out that I had this chain, especially if he fell out with his best friend because of it. I picked it up off the floor and walked into Hannah's bedroom, putting it on the top shelf of her closet where all her shoes would be. This would be the last place he would look. Although we had it good right now, there wasn't no telling the future. Ms. G was holding that donated money for me, and it was strictly for emergency only. This chain could always come in handy if I ended up out on the streets on my ass. It was a lifesaver for me. It would probably save my life one day.

Ahmad

I hadn't spoken to Jayce since our confrontation, and business was going smoothly. Jayce had to get the shipment that I had postponed, and we were continuing to make money. We talked money and nothing more. He was my brother. Although we weren't on our regular level, I was riding for him no matter what. I wasn't up for sucking no man's dick, so I was cool with how we were. It was my week to collect from the traps then distribute shares.

Word was out that there was a fifty-thousand-dollar bounty on Alpo and Rich's head. Usually, that wasn't the way I would've handled the shit, but Jayce and I had two different methods, and since these rats were from his trap, they were his responsibility. They had disappeared, and I wasn't sure if they were in witness protection or if they had really gone AWOL, but again, that was something Jayce was going to have to deal with. All I wanted was for there to be no witnesses, so there would be no case.

As I pulled up to one of the trap buildings, shit was going just as they should've been. The block wasn't hot, which meant more money. I hopped out my whip and entered the building, going to the basement. I knocked on the door four times, a knock that I always did, so they knew it was me. The door swung open, and there was Big Mike standing there with a look of confusion on his face.

"Waddup, fat nigga? You forgot today I collect?" He threw his hands up in surrender.

"Nah, homie, but Jayce already swung by and got the bag. I thought you knew that already," he spoke. I walked into the room without changing my facial expressions.

"Oh aight. I asked that nigga if he could collect from me, and he told me he was busy," I lied.

Jayce and I never spoke on this, and he apparently failed to mention this to me. But I couldn't have my soldiers see that we weren't communicating how we used to. because there was always that one person who tried to step out of line and do some snake shit.

"Oh, aight. He came by like an hour ago. Told me he'd bring the weight later on tonight," he added.

"Aight. Ya sold out, or y'all still got some dope? And how much you gave him?" I questioned. It seemed like I was going to have to ask my own questions because Jayce was moving like a bitch.

"Come on, boss. Don't insult me. When you know this trap to not sell out? Of course, we sold out. We waiting on the drop tonight to re-up and get back to business. He left here with twenty-five thousand," Big Mike said as he looked over at the paper where he wrote down how much he gave.

"Aight, Big Mike. Thanks, bro. That promotion gon' be happening real soon if you keep selling out as fast as you are," I said while walking over to him and giving him a pound before walking over to the door.

He walked behind me and locked the door, and I headed back to the whip. I dialed Jayce's number, and he answered on the first ring.

"Yo."

"Wassup, brother? You collect for me now?" I asked, visibly annoyed in my tone.

"Oh nah, bro. I thought I was just helping you out. I ain't have shit else to do. So much on my mind with this Alpo and Rich shit. I was tryna just switch it up a bit. Nothing against you, bro. I got the bread here," he said. I nodded my head, understanding his point, but I just didn't get why he didn't tell me.

"Aight, bro. Why you ain't put me on? Got a nigga out here looking stupid," I said a little more calmly as I started my car and began to drive off.

"My fault, bro. Shit wasn't about nothing. But yo, we got this problem. Ain't nobody seen these niggas around. What you thinking?" he asked.

If nobody could find Alpo and Rich, there was a good chance witness protection had them, and a nigga had to shake shit up to send a message to them.

"I'll handle it," I said while hanging up the phone. I headed to the pizza shop to pick up the pizza Hannah asked for and headed back to the crib.

It was going on eight o' clock, and the sun was now going down. I walked in the crib, and Hannah was sitting on the couch on her phone, and Honesty was reading a book. Whenever it was quiet, she was reading, something I barely saw most girls do. It was hard to get a bitch to shut up, let alone read a book. I set the pizza on table and headed straight for the bedroom. I changed my clothes, putting on an oversized black Nike Tech sweat suit and black high-top ACG'S. I grabbed two Glocks, putting one in my waistband and one in my ankle. I grabbed a ski mask and headed out the room. Before I walked out the door, Honesty walked over to me and stood in front of me, staring straight into my eyes.

"If Hannah weren't here right now, I'd go with you. Whatever it is your about to do, make it quick, easy, clean, and don't get caught," she said while poking her little manicured finger into my chest. That look in her eye was there again, the same look that drew me to her in the first place.

"I got this, ma. I'll be back in no later than an hour." She stood on her tiptoes and kissed my lips.

"Be safe, Ahmad." She stressed one last time before I walked out.

Me: *Address?*

I texted Jayce, and like clockwork, he texted me right back.

As I drove in silence, I thought about all possible outcomes. Rich's baby mother was Alpo's sister, and she lived right off 145th Street in Harlem projects. When I pulled up, I parked behind the building and grabbed a silencer before opening the broken back door. Like every other project in NYC, all the projects doors were open. I took the steps two at a time while slipping my mask over my face. When I reached the seventeenth floor, I looked down the hall, and there was music blaring. Shit was perfect for right now. I was about to be in and out. I walked down the hall and stopped right in front of her apartment. Her apartment was where all the music was coming from.

I twisted the doorknob, and of course, the door was unlocked. I shook my head because people in the projects just thought they lived somewhere like Beverly Hills and never locked their doors. They got comfortable, forgetting that they were still in the hood, and that anything could happen. It was mostly the women, the ones who thought they knew everybody in their building and trusted the whole block.

I walked in, and the little baby in the bouncer smiled at me, showing his four teeth. He was a spitting image of Rich. I crept in, and the baby bounced higher and higher, smiling and grinning all while drooling. I could smell the aroma of food in the kitchen, and I put my back against the wall. I screwed on my silencer and crept slowly behind the woman who had her back to me. I wrapped my hand around her mouth and put the gun into her side. She tried to scream to no avail. Plus, the music was so loud, no one would hear her.

The baby went from grinning and smiling to bawling like he knew what was going on. I leaned into her ear, so she could hear me over all the noise.

"This is a warning for your snitching ass brother and baby father. The next time I come, you and that baby will be dead. No matter where you go, I will find you. I'll kill any and everyone associated with y'all. It's gon' be a fucking bloodbath," I said while putting a bullet in both her legs before walking out.

And just like that, I was back in my car and driving home like I hadn't just possibly paralyzed a woman. A message like that for Rich and Alpo was sending a clear message. I knew the next time she spoke with them would be means for them to walk away from whatever case the FEDS were building. I didn't make empty threats, and that was something everyone knew about me. If I said I would be back to off everyone in their family, it was most certainly going to happen. I dialed Jayce's number to see if he picked up the shipment and got the answering machine right away.

When I got home, Honesty and I made eye contact, and I nodded my head, reassuring her that everything went smoothly. I rushed straight to the bedroom and stripped out of my clothing and got into the shower. As I washed up, I watched Honesty through the glass with a black bag, throwing the clothes I had just taken off into it. To say I was surprised was an understatement. I lathered my body three times and then got out. She had already pulled out clothes for me. I didn't know if she was doing this out of instinct, or if she was trying to show that she was riding for a nigga, but whatever it was, it was making my dick hard.

My phone received a text, and it was from Syd. I checked, and it was a skull symbol, which meant something went wrong. We had switched our route and routine for shipments since the boys had been on to us, so I knew for sure it couldn't have been them. I dialed Jayce's number again, and it didn't go to voicemail. It was a different message.

"The number you are trying to reach has been disconnected."

And just like that, the pieces to the puzzle made sense. I threw my phone to the floor, shattering it, and began pacing back and forth. Jayce had gotten the shipment and gotten low. I didn't know what the fuck to say, do, or think. I put on some clothes, got strapped up again, and headed out the door. I frantically drove to Jayce's house, hoping that I was just bugging out, and that he was there.

A fifteen-minute drive turned into a three-minute drive. I hopped out the car, leaving it running and rushed to his front door. I looked under the flower pot for his spare key and walked in. Everything looked normal, but I knew exactly what to look for if Jayce was getting the fuck out of dodge. I rushed into his bedroom and to his safe. We both knew each other's safe combo. Just in case something ever happened to one, the other would know where to go to get the bread. When the safe opened, it was cleared out.

"Fuck!" I said under my breath, slamming the safe shut.

I headed out his house without even bothering to lock it. Jayce had fucked me over big time, and I didn't see it. I had given him the benefit of the doubt.

I headed back to the crib, and the minute I pulled up, a car was speeding off. I jumped out while letting bullets go toward the wheel, but they missed. I rushed into the front door that was left open, and Honesty and Hannah were sitting on the floor tied up with tape on their lips. Hannah was crying hysterically while Honesty's eyes were bloodshot red. I took the tape off their lips and rushed to the kitchen to get a knife to undo their restraints.

"It was Jayce!" she yelled.

Once she was untied, I knew exactly what he came here for. I rushed up the stairs and into the office while she untied Hannah. I walked to the closet and just as I thought, my safe had been emptied out. I shook my head from side to side, not even getting angrier at that point. The angrier I allowed myself to be, the more unreasonable I'd be. I sat on the desk with my hands together and shook my head.

He had managed to get low with over a half-million dollars in a day, and I hadn't seen it coming. I didn't know how exactly I was gonna tell Syd and Kai. That my right-hand man that I had vouched for got low with the product, and I couldn't pay them their two hundred thousand?

Syd and Kai were females, but they were just as thorough as a male connect, and they didn't play with their bread, and I didn't blame them. The only thing that was going through my head was finding Jayce, and if Jayce didn't want to be found, he wouldn't be found. Honesty walked into the bedroom, sitting in the chair in between my legs.

"He gon' slip up, and when he does, we gon' be right there to hand it to his ass. Don't stress this," she said, but nothing she could say right now was calming me down.

This nigga was out here acting a fucking fool over a chain that disappeared. Shit was beyond me; the nigga was acting like we weren't brothers. I had finally seen that I had trusted the wrong nigga for all these years. The shit he pulled, I would've never done. But that was neither here nor there. I had to think of something and something fast. I had money stashed up somewhere else that no one knew about, but it was nothing compared to what I had in the safe.

I stood to my feet and headed out the door. It was a moment that I needed to be by myself. Shit was mind-blowing, but I couldn't sit around and bitch about it. I had to think of my next move. I couldn't even make any moves unless I bought a new phone. I took my time driving to the Apple store.

I was gonna find Jayce. He was predictable. He had gotten over on me right now out of anger, but I knew that nigga was happy as fuck, which made him predictable again. I knew exactly what he would try to do next, and when he did try, I would be right there waiting on him, and that was something he wouldn't expect.

Honesty

$\mathcal{I}$ woke up to an empty bed. Yesterday was fucking crazy, and at that point, a bitch was paranoid. Every hour, I was waking up to see if Ahmad had come home and checking on Hannah. I honestly thought Jayce would kill me yesterday, but it seemed like he didn't care about me. His anger was directed toward Ahmad. My stomach was in knots, and I couldn't explain it. I had an adrenaline rush. This shit had me scared but feeling good. I knew I was watching too much *Power* on Starz. Shit, I was feeling like Angela. Ahmad was Ghost, and Jayce's stupid ass was Tommy. I chuckled at the thought of how ironic this shit was.

The smell of food crept into the bedroom, and for some reason, I thought that maybe Ahmad was home, but when I got downstairs, it was Hannah cooking. Ms. G had rubbed off on her. She had made a small breakfast for three—a platter of eggs, pancakes, bacon, and biscuits. This, I could get used to.

"Ohhhh, lil' sis, can you cook like this every day!" I said playfully, trying to brighten up the room.

There was a little tension, and I really didn't know what to say to her about what happened yesterday.

"Nope. I start school on Monday. Thank God. Some kind of normalcy in my life," she stated in a serious tone.

"Han, I'm sorry," I said, walking beside her.

"Honesty, I like Ahmad, but not enough for me to put my life on the line for him. If yesterday is your preference on how to live, give me a choice on how to live my life. Momma would've never subjected us to something like that, so why you wanna live this life?" she said, staring at me.

Her words stung, and I was ashamed because she was right. This wasn't our lifestyle, and who was I to drag her into a life I wanted to live with this man? I hadn't asked her once what she preferred and realized that I was dragging her into whatever I dragged myself into.

"You're right, Hannah, and I'm really sorry. I haven't been considerate of you, but that ends here. What is it you really want to do?" I asked, knowing what she'd say, but I couldn't even be mad at her. I was barely eighteen trying to parent my little sister.

"I wanna stay with Ms. G, and I can come here on the weekends instead," she suggested. It was a hard pill to swallow, and I had nothing to say, so I nodded my head.

"I'll talk to her about it," I said while walking back out the kitchen. I stopped when she responded.

"I spoke to her this morning, and she said no problem."

My heart sank in my chest. Was I really doing so bad that it made her take matters into her own hands? I wanted to beg her to stay with me but knew it was selfish to ask. She had given me a chance, and I had blew it, so it was time to let her decide for herself. And I couldn't act like her decision was a bad one, because it wasn't.

I had no worries when it came to Hannah living with Ms. G. She was literally like our second mother. And had been there for us when we had no one. I trusted Ms. G with my life, and I knew our mother did as well.

I went back upstairs to the bedroom to catch a break from this shit with Ahmad yesterday and with Hannah wanting to leave. I was starting to feel like everything was my fault. Had I not taken the chain that day, Ahmad and Jayce wouldn't be beefing, and he wouldn't have ran up in here and scared Hannah shitless and back to Ms. G's house. I wanted so badly to tell Ahmad about the chain, so we could have some kind of money, but I was scared of the outcome of revealing the truth.

I had lied to him so much about not knowing Jayce and taking the chain that I knew that revealing the truth would do more damage. I couldn't do more damage. I had lost my mother. I was losing Hannah, and I couldn't lose him too. I wouldn't allow it. The chain would go to the grave with me if I had to. I picked up my phone and dialed Ahmad's phone, and after ringing twice, he sent me to voicemail. I wasn't calling for anything else except to hear his voice. It might've been selfish at a time like this with everything he had going on, but I had shit going on too.

I put the phone down and a text came through from him.

Ahmad: *Stay at Ms. G house this weekend with Hannah, lay low.*

I just sent a thumbs up. I took a quick shower, got dressed, packed clothes for the weekend, and went downstairs.

"Hannah, pack your things, so we can go!" I shouted from the kitchen, so she could hear me in her bedroom.

I made a plate and sat down and ate. Shit, Hannah cooked better than me hands down. I couldn't help but to eat mine and Ahmad's portion. From the looks of it, he wasn't coming home any time soon anyway, so I might as well have helped myself. After eating the majority of the food, Hannah finally came down.

"Damn, girl. You act like you ain't ate in weeks," she said jokingly, while looking at me with a mouthful of food.

"Shut up. You put your foot, your back, your neck, and everything else up in this," I complimented, which caused her to laugh.

I ordered an Uber from my phone and waited for our driver to arrive.

"Shit, I need to learn how to drive with all this Uber business. They getting hella money outta me," I complained, but it was the truth. If Ahmad wasn't around, I was taking Uber everywhere. I ain't have it like that. I was two seconds away from using the buses and trains again.

When our Uber got there, we hopped in, and I sent Naomi a text letting her know we were on our way. I knew she'd be all extra and excited. The girl cried for God's sake when I moved out, acting like I moved out of state.

When we got to the house, Ms. G was cooking, and I could smell her cooking from outside. My stomach was grumbling like I hadn't just ate 75 percent of the food that Hannah had made. I figured I was just being greedy at that point.

Greedy ain't never hurt nobody, I thought to myself.

We stepped in the house, and Hannah ran over to Ms. G, giving her a big hug. I chuckled to myself.

"Y'all are so dramatic! It's been two days," I said, laughing.

Ms. G shooed me away. "Don't be jealous."

I continued laughing while walking into Nay's room where there was music blasting. When I walked in, she was making her twerking video. I shook my head because this bitch couldn't stop twerking if her life depended on it. I walked into her video and began twerking with her. This only added more fuel to her fire, and of course, she had to outdo me. I laughed while getting out the video and letting her finish doing her thing. After about five minutes, she finally turned the music down and lay beside me on her bed.

"Bitch, you here for the weekend? Oh, it's lit! Trick is throwing a party tomorrow night at Lorraine's. We out," she said, overly excited, but I was about to burst her bubble when I turned her down.

"Girl, I'm not going to Lorraine's. The whole damn club smell like cheap perfume, cheap weave, and hookah. I'll pass," I said, scrunching my face up.

"Come on, please!" she begged, and my answer was still no.

Ahmad never told me to stay away from anyone since I had met him, and Trick was the first. He hadn't told me the reason, but his judgment was all I needed to stay away.

"Aight, hoe. Well, we can go get our hair and feet done because you are looking rough," she joked while putting her hand through my messy hair.

"Fuck you, bitch," I said, laughing. I knew she was right.

I hadn't gotten my hair done since my birthday, and it was well over-due, especially because a bitch was lowkey moping. A little pampering always did make shit better. Then the thought of being robbed by Jayce crossed my mind. I had some money, but the little money I did have I had to use wisely.

"On you?" I asked while raising an eyebrow.

"Of course not! On Trick Daddy, hoe!" she beamed, and I shrugged my shoulders.

Shit, if he was spoiling her like that, then fuck it. My hair did need some doing, and my nails were lifting.

"You find out what he do?" I asked skeptically again. I was hoping she'd say yes.

"Yeah, girl. He's a sponsor pretty much. The nigga just be out here flossing and giving hoes money," she said, and in my head, all I could think was *that nigga a pimp.*

I didn't know how Nay got sponsor from pimp, or maybe she just didn't know what she was talking about. I shrugged my shoulders and sat back on the bed. The way Nay was tripping over this dude, I really wanted to know about him. I sat back, and she walked over to her desk and pulled out a rock and metro card, making lines.

"Nay, are you fucking serious!" I said, jumping off the bed and spinning her chair toward me.

"Girl, why you tripping. I done it a few times with Trick, and a bitch get higher than a kite. Pussy be wetter than an ocean. Ain't no big deal." She tried to convince me, and I was completely baffled.

She was doing shit we had laughed at other bitches for doing, switching up on herself over a nigga. I was pissed at that point. When they said bad things came in three's, that shit was definitely the truth. First, Ahmad, then Hannah, and now, Naomi. I had a feeling she was more into Trick for more than she was letting on, but I was going to get to the bottom of it.

"I'll go to Lorraine's with you tomorrow if you put this shit away and don't do it in front of me again, Nay, and I mean that shit."

She sniffed a line and then nodded her head.

"Deal, bitch. Look, I'm putting it away," she said after sniffing another line in her nostril.

I wanted to tackle her to the ground, but that would only cause Ms. G to come up in here, and I knew that if Ms. G knew what the fuck was going on, Naomi would be homeless. Ms. G didn't ask for much, just to respect her and her home, and she provided and gave Naomi everything. There was no way in hell she was standing for this. She put it away, and anger boiled in me as I watched her nod off at the head. She was looking identical to a crackhead, and I was speechless. I couldn't believe my eyes. I was trying to understand when did she start this? Did me moving out cause her to try new shit like this? What the hell had happened? I was coming up with nothing. She had never told me about this, and I knew she knew better than that, but she was sniffing lines like she had been doing it for a minute, and all I could think was I had to get near Trick and see what the fuck he was about. Obviously, he had Nay on some different type of time. There was a time where Nay and I would always say we couldn't understand bitches who did coke, and here she was.

Ahmad

*J*ayce sat in a closed-up section of the club, flaunting bread that wasn't his, smoking weed, and buying bottles that he wouldn't finish. The minute I had left the crib, a lightbulb had went off in my head. I knew the nigga was going to get out of dodge but not before going to see his mom's gravesite. When I got there, all kinds of thoughts went in my head, but I knew to play it smart. There was no way in hell that he was riding dirty with product and all that bread that he took. I followed him for an entire day, and the cat and mouse games was enough for me. Syd had been blowing me up. We had spoken once, and I let her know I was handling it. This messy ass nigga had taken out two of her men and drove off with the money and the coke. He was on some movie shit, and I didn't understand why the nigga thought he was about to be moving around like El Chapo. I played the back of the club and asked the owner, Mr. Reese, to shut the doors down. This wasn't the first time the old man was doing me a favor. The compensation after doing favors for me was lovely. So he played by the streets. He ain't see shit, ain't hear shit, so there must've never been no shit.

The dancer in front of Jayce had him so distracted that he didn't feel my presence behind him. I took out my pistol and hit him in his temple hard enough to knock him out but soft enough to keep him alive. I grabbed the duffle bag of money he'd been flaunting in the club. I wanted everything back, and I knew he wasn't gonna give it up easily. I tied his hands and feet with zip ties and dragged him out the back door, placing him in the trunk of a stolen car that had been doused with ammonia.

I drove to a warehouse that Jay and I had taken many people to get the truth out of them, and it hurt a nigga heart that I was bringing his ass there for switching up and being disloyal.

When I pulled up, I pulled out my gun again and popped the trunk open. I watched as he struggled to get some fresh air while keeping his eyes closed because of the ammonia.

"Nigga, you might as well bury me now. 'Cause a nigga not giving you shit," he said cockily. It was expected of him.

I didn't say a word. I picked him up and dragged him inside, laying him on the cold metal table. I hit him in the head again to knock him out, so I could restrain him to the table without having to fight with him. When I felt his body go limp, I took the zip ties off his legs and strapped them to the table. And did the same for his hands. Once I was done, I picked up the bleach bottle that was sitting in the corner and splashed some on his face. I wanted him to wake the fuck up and be in pain when he did.

"Arrrgghhh!" he yelled.

It was time for answers, and I wasn't going to leave here until I got them.

"My nigga, you know me well enough to know that all I want to know is where the product and money is. Then I'll let you go, and you can disappear," I said calmly, staring at his bloodshot eyes. He let out a laugh then spat on my shoes.

"Fuck you, nigga! You gon' have to kill me then deal with the fact that Kai and Syd still gon' kill you and your bitch if you don't get them the bread."

I didn't say another word. The human body could only take but so much pain before people began telling the truth. I knew this because it is wasn't my first go round.

Before I was deep into the drug game, torturing a motherfucker was my thing. With a new status in these streets, I decided to lay low and let other people handle problems like this for me. But it wasn't nothing for a nigga to come out of retirement. Plus, there was no one that I could get to do this job in particular for me. Motherfuckers out here feared Jayce just as much as they feared me. I could only imagine having someone else do this job for me and Jayce having them bitch up and get away. There was too much at stake, and I needed to be the one to handle it. I loved Jayce like a brother, and even the mere thought of having to treat him like an outsider made me feel funny, but it was a dog eat dog world, and he had shown me that with the shit he pulled. He had done the ultimate betrayal.

I sharpened one of the scalpels that sat on the wall full of weapons and pulled a chair up to sit in front of him. I didn't want to do this to him, but there wasn't no choice. I had to just put it in my head this wasn't my brother. The Jayce I had known for years wasn't this man in front of me. In front of me was a nigga who wanted smoke, and it was smoke I was going to give him. The things niggas didn't understand was that too much smoke could kill you, and it was the person who started the fire's fault.

"Make sure you kill me, nigga. 'Cause if you don't, I'mma go back and kill that bitch and her sister," he threatened.

His words went in one ear and out the other. This shit was redundant. I had heard all this shit before from previous niggas, and I wasn't fazed by it one bit. I raised from my seat and walked over to one of his hands.

"Speak now or forever hold your peace," I said as I took my time cutting the lines on his index finger until there was no more finger left.

"Ahhhh!" he yelled in pain. "Fuck you, Ahmad!"

I grabbed the bottle of ammonia and put his entire hand in it. I knew with Jayce being as stubborn as he was, I was going to have to take my time. The pain of the ammonia eating up his fingers caused him to pass out. That was another thing. The human body could only take so much pain before passing out, but there was no time for that. I used the remote that controlled the movement of the table and pressed a button until his head was upside down. I grabbed a bucket out the corner and poured bleach inside, adding a little water in it to dilute. Killing him was easy. Getting the answers out of him was the hard part. After filling the bucket up, I placed it under his head and watched as he began shaking and fighting for air. After fifteen seconds of fighting, I removed the bucket, and he began coughing and choking.

"Come on, man. Just tell me where my shit is, and we can go about our business."

I tried to negotiate, but Jayce knew just as well as I knew that he wasn't leaving here whether he told me where the product and money was at or not. He had fucked up the brotherhood, and letting him go meant having to watch my back for the rest of my life, and that wasn't something

I was fond of. So either way, he was going to die. The only choice that he had was whether it would be quick and easy or slow and painful.

"That's all you got, nigga? I need my toes done too, bro," he said mockingly.

"Your wish is my command," I said, walking over to the wall and grabbing a butcher knife.

His eyes widened as I walked back over to him. His cockiness let me know I was letting him off easy, and it was because of the history, but we would see who was going to be laughing. I laid the table down, so he would be laying flat and picked the knife up above my head. Using all the force I had, I cut down through the bone on his ankle.

"Ahhhhhh!" he screamed in agony, but that didn't stop me from raising my hand up and cutting off his other foot.

The blood instantly began spewing out, and his piercing scream echoed throughout the place. I moved the bucket from the head of the table to the foot of the table and switched the table to stand upward. This wasn't a game, and I wasn't trying to be here all day. The blood from his nubs turned the color of the bleach and water a crimson red.

"I'll tell you! I will tell you where it's at! Please, just stop!" he yelled, and I moved the bucket.

"Talk, nigga," I said, and he began coughing and trying to catch his breath. "It's… It's in… It's in your dead mother's pussy," he said while forming a smile, revealing the blood in his mouth.

I shook my head and turned around as if I was going to walk away, but I pulled my gun back out and beat him across the mouth with it. It was the first time in my twenty-two years of life that I had actually witnessed teeth failing out someone's mouth. I stopped and just sat back. It was time for me to think of another plan. Jayce wasn't going to let up and tell me shit, and I knew that well enough. Torturing him wasn't giving me the adrenaline rush it used to give me. All I was worried about was the coke and bread, and I just had to think fast. I was ready to put him out his misery but not without adding pain.

I grabbed the bat off the wall that had nails sticking out of it and began beating on his body until it became mush forty-five minutes later. Jayce had died within the first twenty minutes, but he had me frustrated like that. I didn't stop hitting on the body until I thought of a way to get the money and product. I had some money from what he had at the club, but it was nowhere near enough to pay for the product. And even if I did pay for the product, what was I gonna have to live off of? In every scenario, I was coming up short, and the only thing that it seemed like I could do at the moment was stall Syd and Kai, but stalling would only go but so far. With the time that I did have, I needed to think of a plan and think of it fast.

I walked out the warehouse with blood all over my clothing and hopped in the stolen car. I drove to the crib, and as I drove, I called Big Mike.

"Yo, boss," he answered.

"The warehouse on Hunts Point needs cleaning. Get your boys to clean it up. And come by the crib and dispose of this whip," I said, hanging up. I wasn't in no mood to have a discussion.

I got to the house and grabbed the bag of money I had taken from Jayce. I walked in the crib, and I knew Honesty and Hannah wasn't there. That was a good thing. I had too much blood on me and didn't want nobody questioning me. I hopped in the shower and watched as my best friend's blood rinsed down the drain. I didn't feel bad. He had made himself the enemy. Shit didn't have to go the way it went down. Jayce's ego and pride was what brought his demise.

After twenty minutes of making sure there was no more blood or Jayce's DNA on me, I got out the shower and wrapped a towel on my waist. Only thing on my mind was finding out how much money was in the bag. I didn't even bother to put clothes on. I flipped the money out the back and began counting. After thirty minutes and counting twice to make sure I was accurate, there was one hundred and fifty thousand in the bag. It was half of what was owed the Syd and Kai, and even if I gave that up, what was I gonna live off? I had three mouths to feed, and being broke wasn't an option.

I put the money in the bag and walked to Hannah's room. I went into the closet that she didn't really use and threw the bag up there. The next time someone thought they were going to ransack my place, they wouldn't expect a kid's room to be where the little stash I had was left.

Honesty

Naomi and I walked through the doors of club Lorraine, and like I said, cheap weave that smelled like it had been burned by flat irons and cheap Victoria's Secret perfume could be smelled throughout the place. Of course, you couldn't miss the smell of the hookah that every bitch in there had and was smoking. I shook my head as Nay walked in, bobbing her head to the music, and I looked around in disgust.

I was the last person to think I was better than anybody, but even when I was dirt poor, you couldn't pay me to come to this spot. The whole room was like a moving STD. Shit, I wasn't trying to rub shoulders with none of these hoes and get bedbugs. I was mad as hell that I was in there. Naomi spotted Trick and grabbed my hand and walked over to him. On his lap was two girls and four other bitches sitting around. I thought Nay would walk over and punch one of them hoes in the nose, knowing I had her follow up, but she didn't. She waved to them hoes and sat right beside them. The look on my face said enough, and Nay could tell.

"Chill, Honesty," she said while trying to pull me down to sit beside her, but I refused.

"I'll stand," I said, while looking around.

Naomi even wanting to be in this setting had me baffled. We used to chase the big bucks, and the niggas in here didn't look like they had shit else to offer except STD's, baby mama drama, and headaches, and I was gonna pass on that. I looked at Trick, and he was grinning from ear to ear, feeling like the man. I watched as a man came up to him and nodded at Naomi, and Trick leaned over and whispered in her ear, which caused her to fake a giggle, stand up, and grab the man's hand. I grabbed her other hand to stop her from going. Just like I thought, this nigga was pimping these bitches out and giving them materialistic shit to make them feel worthy.

"Nay, you better fucking not. I promise you I will turn this place upside the fuck down," I said loud enough for everyone to hear me. She looked at me like I was embarrassing her.

"Honesty, you doing too much. I'm grown, sis. Chill out," she said, grilling me before walking to the back.

I wanted to kick, fight, scream, and even leave the damn place, but I'd be damned if I left without her. That wasn't even an option for me. We came together, and we damn sure were going to be leaving together. Whatever Naomi did on her own personal time, I was gonna leave her to it, but while we were together, we were going to stick together.

After about an hour passed, all the bitches that were flocking on Trick's lap had walked off with different men to the back room. I was really beginning to wonder how fucking big that damn room was. He sat there eyeing me like he was preying on me, and he had no idea that he couldn't get next to me.

"Nigga, you might have these bitches wrapped around your little ass dick, but a bitch like me ain't pressed over you," I spat, so he would know I wasn't fond of his fake Katt Williams looking ass.

He chuckled and stood up and walked over to me, standing real close like he didn't know what personal space was.

"Baby, ain't nothing little about this dick," he said while whipping it out right in the middle of the little club, not caring who saw. "I'm a businessman. They my ladies. I take care of 'em. Don't hate the playa; hate the game," he said, sounding like a fucking clown to me.

I grilled him so hard that if looks could kill, he'd be buried in the dirt. I looked around the club. I was getting impatient waiting for Nay. I was ready to go, and whether she was done or not, she was walking out this bitch with me the same way we had came in. I walked toward the back room that I had seen everyone else walk through, and it was like Lorraine's had its own little bando connected to it. I walked down the hall, making turns and finally following the sounds of moans.

When I finally reached the room, the taste of throw up was in the back of my throat. Inside were little twin sized beds on the floor, and everybody fucking one another, not giving a damn who saw. I scanned the big warehouse, looking in each room for Nay, and I finally found her. She was bent over with a whole different dude than she had walked away with, and his dick was raw in her ass. She looked up at me with glossy eyes and a smile as she moaned while he pumped in and out of her.

"Aww, baby. I'm about to cum," the man on top of her moaned.

I pulled out my phone and dialed Ahmad. He answered on the first ring, and I was grateful.

"Mhad, please come pick me up. I'm at Lorraine's," I said in one breath as my heart began beating fast.

"What the fuck you doing there! Get the fuck out! I'm coming!" he yelled into my ear.

At this point, I knew he knew what the fuck was going on, and I would take all the yelling he would do as long as that meant getting the fuck out of here. I walked over to Nay and snatched her arm up, looking for the shorts and crop top she came in with. The man who was fucking her in the ass looked over at me and yelled.

"Give me my bitch back!" he yelled, and I ignored him because I could give a fuck about what he was saying.

Nay was feeling like dead weight as I tried putting her clothes on. I couldn't find her panties, and she was nodding off. I was just ready to get the fuck up out of here. As I finally got her clothes on, Trick walked into the room with the guy who was having his way with Nay beside him.

"Aht, aht," he said with a smile on his face.

"Nigga, fuck you," I said, walking by him and dragging Nay by one of her hands. He pulled her other hand and walked closer to her.

"Baby, you leaving me?" he said to Nay in a childish voice, and she snatched her hand away from me and fell onto his chest.

"Oh no, daddy. I'm not going nowhere," she said with her head in his chest.

"Oh, yes the fuck you are," I said, grabbing her hand back. She snatched her hand back and stood beside Trick.

"Honesty, let's go!" Ahmad's voice boomed through the room, causing me to jump a bit.

"I'm not leaving her," I said without breaking eye contact with her.

When my stare got to be too much, she looked away, and Trick turned her away from me, and they walked away. I ran up behind him, hitting him in the head, and he raised his hand like he was about to pimp slap me like I was pretty sure he did his bitches. Ahmad caught his hand right in the air while pulling his gun out and pointing it at him.

"I don't think you wanna do that, bro," he said, and Trick pulled his arm away and continued walking with Nay.

Ahmad grabbed my hand and dragged me out the whore house and to the car. I couldn't help but cry. I was upset and angry, and there was nothing I could do. Nay was gone, and there was nothing I could do about it and that made me frustrated.

"Didn't I fucking tell you to stay away from that nigga?" Ahmad yelled as he drove away.

I had nothing to say. The tears that ran from my eyes wouldn't allow me to talk. Nay was not only my best friend, but she was my blood sister. She was so far gone, and I didn't know how I didn't see it. I cared about her the same way I cared about Hannah. I felt like the most horrible sister in the world at that point. The ears continued falling, and I couldn't even catch my breath.

"Stop the car!" I yelled while opening the door, and Ahmad pressed his foot hard on the breaks causing the car to jerk.

I hopped out, and the throw up that had been sitting in the back of my throat came up as I vomited. Ahmad got out the car and held my hair up while rubbing my back. To say I was disgusted was an understatement. After catching my breath, I took a seat in the car trying to gain my composure.

"I stayed away like you said, but Nay didn't. She been fucking with him since the party," I said, shaking my head from side to side.

"Nay is her own women, ma. You can't take that burden and put it on yourself. I watched as she picked him instead of you, and there's no coming back from that," he said in a calm tone.

The tears invaded my eyes again and began to fall. "She's my sister; my blood, Ahmad," I said barely above a whisper, but I knew he heard me because he turned his head to look at me. He shook his head again as if he was speechless.

"How am I supposed to tell Ms. G?"

"You don't. All that's gonna do is break her heart," he said, and he was right, but I knew I had to say something. We had left the house together, and she needed an explanation.

"I have to. I'll figure out the right words before saying anything," I said while putting my head back and enjoying the ride home.

It was about two in the morning, and I was beat and exhausted. I just wanted to get Nay's situation out of my head, but I couldn't. I kept thinking of ways to tell Ms. G but kept coming up short. There was no nice way to tell her that her daughter was strung out on drugs. When we pulled up to the house, I let Ahmad go in before me. I wasn't going to rest until I spoke with Ms. G. I dialed her number, and on the third ring, she answered.

"Baby, is everything okay?" she asked, and I couldn't help it as the tears began coming down again.

"It's Nay, Ms. G. She's doing drugs and refused to come home," I said in between tears, not giving all the details.

I couldn't bring myself to let her know that Nay was a prostitute. It was something I couldn't fix my lips to say. Ms. G took a deep sigh on her end of the phone.

"Baby, just pray for her. That's the only thing we can do. I been praying for her. I noticed a change in her but didn't know what," she said in a sad voice. "Stop crying. When she wants help, she knows where to find us. Don't burden yourself with that," she said, trying to calm me down. I didn't know how she could be so calm. Her daughter was out here carrying on as a crackhead, and she was calm. "I'll talk to you tomorrow, baby. I'm about to pray, and you should do the same."

I nodded my head as if she could see me and hung up the phone. I got out the car and entered the house, and Ahmad was sitting on the couch smoking a blunt, something he rarely did. He only did it when he was stressed, and he didn't allow anyone to stress him out, so this was something out of the ordinary.

"What's on your mind?" I said, walking over and leaning on the arm of the couch.

"I killed Jay," he said nonchalantly, and my heart sank.

It wasn't because I felt bad, but I kind of felt like what we were going through was my fault. Shit had gone too far. I could tell that was half the reason why, but something else was on his mind.

"What else?" I asked, trying to get it out of him.

"Still don't have the product nor all the money. I gotta think of a plan and quick. Trying to flip one hundred thousand to half a mil in a week... shit is almost impossible, but I gotta pull it off."

"Whatever the plan is, count me in. I'll be your right-hand man," I said before walking up the stairs toward the bedroom.

"I love you," he said, and I stopped in my tracks. I looked at him as he blew smoke out his mouth while looking at me.

"I love you too, Ahmad," I replied, continuing up the stairs.

My heart fluttered, jumped, and flipped. This was the first time we'd both said: "I love you." The way I felt was all mushy inside. This was the first time any man had told me he loved me and the first time I had said it to any man in my life. I knew I loved Ahmad, but actually saying the words out my mouth was a different feeling. The fact that he had said it first had taken me by surprise. He had managed to make a bad night feel like one of the best nights in the world.

I stripped out of my clothing and put them in the trashcan in the bathroom right where they belonged. I got into the steaming hot shower and tried to scrub away the disgust that I felt. The sight of Nay high and taking dick in her ass gave me the urge to vomit again. I had to do everything in my power to push Nay to the back of my head. I was going to do exactly what Ms. G said to do in hopes that it worked. I scrubbed my skin until it felt sore and stood as the burning water rinsed off my body. I got out and just looked in the mirror. My eyes were swollen from all the crying I had done.

I lotioned my skin with my strawberry scented body oil. Ahmad and I both had a rough night, and I didn't want to sleep feeling the way I felt. I wanted to feel good, and what better way was it to do that than to smell good and be up under my man? I put on a lingerie set that I had ordered off Fashion Nova. The first time I had tried it on, it was slightly big, but this shit fit the fuck out of me when I put it on. I took a hair clip and pinned my hair up before kneeling beside the bed and closing my eyes. I sat with my eyes closed and hands together for about a minute then opened them and realized I hadn't prayed since my mother was alive. Prayer hadn't worked then, so why would it work now? I wanted to just get up off the floor and go downstairs to Ahmad, but my conscious wouldn't let me. Nay needed me, and if there was a chance this could work, then I at least had to try. I tried gathering my thoughts before closing my eyes again.

"Um... Dear God, the last time I prayed, you didn't answer my prayer, because obviously, my mother isn't here right now. So I don't know if I caught you at a bad time then or around a time you were unavailable, but I just hope if this message is going through your voice-mail that you hear it really soon. I need you too look over Nay and guide her back home. She got that monkey on her back, and if anyone can help her, it's you, ain't it? Okay. Thank you, and um, continue to look over Hannah, Ms. G, and Ahmad. I can't lose anyone else. My heart just won't take it. Amen. Thank you. Bye," I said before standing on my two feet.

I turned to face the door, and Ahmad stood there and chuckled.

"I ain't know God got a voicemail. That's some new shit I ain't heard of," he said, causing me to laugh and brightening up the mood. It may not have been the perfect prayer, but I just hoped it was a prayer that worked.

THE FOLLOWING MORNING, I woke up with the urge to vomit. My body was drenched in sweat I had been tossing and turning all night. I turned to my side, and of course, Ahmad wasn't there. I knew he had shit to handle. Jayce had really fucked us up. I rushed out the bed and barely made it to the toilet as I vomited all over the seat. All night I had dreams, or should I say nightmares? They were about Nay, and it really wasn't sitting well with me.

That prayer I had said last night... I was hoping that God had heard it and was working on answering it. My stomach was feeling queasy, and I couldn't put a finger on it. I rose to the sink and began brushing my teeth. I washed my face and just stared at myself. I was looking eighteen alright. My face was getting bigger, I had bags under my eyes, and I swear I was starting to gain some weight in all the right places. Shit, I'd take the weight gain over the fat face and baggy eyes. If this was what being eighteen looked like, I was going have to pass. I walked back into the bedroom, and my phone was sitting on the bed ringing. It was Ms. G, and before I answered, I had my fingers crossed that she was calling to give me some good news about Nay's ass coming home.

"Hello," I answered.

"Hey, little girl. Guess what?" she said, and all I could think was *Thank you, God for answering my prayer. Nay is home.* But as always, it seemed like Ms. G was some kind of mind reading old lady because she continued talking.

"Nay isn't back yet, baby. Be patient prayer takes time. The news is I dreamed of fishes," she said, and to say I was confused said the least.

"Ms. G, no offense, but you called me 'cause you dreamt of food?" I rolled my eyes and shook my head.

"Little girl, watch who you talking to. Just 'cause you about to be a mother don't mean you gonna be out here talking to me any kind of way. I pop grown kids too. Don't play with me," she ranted.

I knew I had it coming, but where was she getting her intel from? I didn't have a clue because wasn't nobody pregnant over here. Her threat caused me to chuckle because I knew she meant it.

"Whose about to be a mother? Who told you this? 'Cause they a lie."

"Little girl, its either you or that damn drugged up sister of yours. One of y'all little fast butts is pregnant. I know it. I know. I know it. Anytime I dream of fish, it's correct. Dreamed of it with your mama and dreamed of it with my damn self. I know it's one of y'all," she said in a calmer tone, sounding more confident than ever. "Ohhh, I'm about to be a grandma!" she yelled excitedly, and all I could do was laugh.

I was completely convinced Ms. G had found Nay's stash and did a few lines because something had to give. Even the mere thought of Ms. G doing lines made me crack up in laughter.

"Girl, bring your ass over here. I'm going to get a test to find out if it's you or Naomi. If its Nay, that'll give me a reason to snatch her little fast ass up by the ear and bring her home. Hurry up," She said, hanging up without taking no for an answer.

I didn't mind at that point because if proving I wasn't pregnant meant she was going to go get Nay, then I was going to do it.

I put on a pencil skirt, a camisole and some furry slides then requested my Uber to Ms. G's house. I was in a better mood knowing that Ms. G was serious. Ms. G was known for being a wild one back in the day, and that was why everyone knew and respected Nay and I nor did they mess with us. Everyone knew if they messed with her girls, she was coming outside with a bat and a chain and fucking everything up in site. I hadn't witnessed her beating ass with my own eyes, but the way people respected her, I knew it wasn't a bluff.

I rushed out the house once my Uber came. You would've thought I was on my way to a dick appointment from the way I was acting, but nope. I was happy that I was about to get my sister back. When I walked in the door, Ms. G wasted no time. She grabbed my arm, pushed me into the bathroom, and two pregnancy sticks sat on the sink. They weren't the dollar store kind either. They were the ones that printed the word *pregnant* on it if you were, and it could tell you up to five days early. I chuckled and shook my head. She wasn't playing around with this dream.

I peed on the stick and washed my hands and waited for the results. Once the two minutes passed, I looked down at it, and my heart dropped to my ass.

"No! No! No!" I whispered to myself, panicking.

I opened the other box, and even though there was no pee left in me, I forced until something came out. The first one had to be malfunctioning. There was no way I was pregnant. I sat on the toilet with the test in my hands, waiting for the results to pop up, and again, the word *pregnant* popped up.

Ahmad

"Ahmad, it's been a week, and we still ain't got no bread. We gave you time that we wouldn't have given anybody else, and now, it seems like you just don't give a fuck. That's the problem with this business right now and the reason Syd and I are stuck in our ways. We let a nigga slide, and he start ice skating. Ain't much more we can do for you. So have our bread by tonight, or bodies gon' start dropping. We've been doing business long enough for you to know that once bodies start dropping, they ain't gon' stop till we get our money," Kai spoke into the phone.

I knew in my head there wasn't no way in hell I was going to have her bread by the night, so I tried negotiating.

"Listen, you right, and the shit going on ain't got shit to do with you. You know as well as I know that I'm good enough for this extension. I got twenty-five bands right now that I can have my men bring to you, but I need more time."

"Time is money, brother man. Time is something you no longer have," she said before hanging up. I walked out the office and into Hannah's room.

All week, I had thought of how to flip one hundred bands to half a mil, and it was impossible with no connect. So a nigga was going to have to make what he could and lay low. Syd and Kai were true to their word and would deliver, taking me out meant no bread for them, so that meant they were going to be on a hunt for everyone who worked for me. Good thing about it was my guys were always ready for whatever smoke that came their way. I wasn't going to leave them for dead. I was definitely about to put them all up on game. I picked up my phone, sending an alarm symbol to Big Mike.

94

Big Mike: *Say less.*

That was it. My job was done. We had protocol set in place for war, and once that text was sent out, everybody was going to be on their A game. I did my part. It was just time to flip this money. I walked to Hannah's room and pulled the bag down from her closet. When the bag came down, so did the root of all evil. Jayce's chain; the one Honesty claimed she had no idea about was here in this room. To say I was shocked was an understatement. I was speechless. This chain was what started the chain of events that caused us to be in this predicament. I went from surprised to pissed in 2.5 seconds. I stormed out the room and into the kitchen where Honesty was cooking. With her back to me, she could hear my footsteps.

"Babe, I got news for you." She turned around, and the chain in my hand caused her jaw to drop to the ground.

"I can exp—" She tried to speak, but it was like my hand had a mind of its own.

I wrapped it around her neck and began to squeeze. I wanted to squeeze the life out of her. She kicked and scratched and tried to release my grip, but I refused to let up. I wanted her to know this was it. I wanted her to know that if I ever saw her again, I would kill her. This was over between us, and I wanted her to know that without me even expressing it. I had tried to bring her into my life and show her something different without asking for nothing from her, except loyalty and honesty. But that she couldn't deliver, and I was hurt. I felt her body about to go limp and let go of her.

"Get out," I said like I hadn't just almost ended her life, and she began sobbing.

"Ahmad, I'm sorry. I'm so sorry." She cried from the kitchen floor.

I walked away without looking back. A nigga's heart was hurting. Her cries were so piercing and painful that I wanted to go pick her up off the floor and console her, but I couldn't. My pride wouldn't let me. I had killed my best friend over her deceit. There was a war starting because of her, and all she had to do was be honest with a nigga, and she couldn't even do that. She cried harder and louder, and I couldn't take it no more. I walked back into the kitchen, and she looked up at me with fearful eyes, scrambling on to get away from me. The sight alone was tearing a nigga apart. She was my weakness, and she didn't even know it. The fear in her eyes was evident, and I looked away, grabbing her and dragging her to the door while she kicked and screamed and tried to fight me.

"Noooo! I'm not leaving! I'm pregnant!" she screamed, and a part of me didn't want her to leave.

A part of me wanted her to keep fighting to stay, so I could have a reason to let her stay. That same part of me wanted to believe that she really was pregnant, but I knew the truth. She was saying anything just to let me have her stay, and I just knew I couldn't. The angel on my right shoulder was telling me let her go to at least get some of her belongings, and the devil on the left told me that she didn't but anything in this house. The devil was right.

I opened the door, and just as I went to put her outside, I noticed Tiana was standing there with Quan in her arms and a big smile spread across her face. She looked over at Honesty, who was in tears with her hair a mess and smirked. It must have been an ego thing because Honesty stopped fighting and stood on her two feet and walked past Tiana, bumping her on the shoulder. I wanted to grab her and tell her don't go and come back so that we could fix it, but I couldn't have what I wanted at that moment. The truth was that we couldn't fix it.

"What do you want, T?" I asked, not wanting to let her in.

"I'm pregnant," she said loud and clear.

I looked behind her at Honesty, wondering if she heard, and when she turned around and looked at me like her world had shattered, I knew she did. I hated that I had to hurt her for her to understand that what she did to me was fucked up. I stepped aside, letting Tiana in and took one last look at Honesty before closing the door. I didn't know who I was hurting more behind my actions, her or myself. I walked over to the couch and stared at Jay's chain on the table. That little as chain was what had us in this situation. I shook my head from side to side, and Tiana cleared her throat, trying to get my attention.

"What do you want, Tiana?" I asked again.

I was hoping that she changed her reason for being here and what she said outside was just to get under Honesty's skin.

"Oh, you thought I was playing? Nah, potnah. I'm pregnant, pregnant," she said, laughing like it was it a joke.

I looked at her with a serious face, because even if she was pregnant, the damn baby wasn't mine.

"Last time I checked, you and Jay was fucking, Tee. Stop playing with me. We ain't fucked in about two months. You not about to come up in here and pin no seed on me."

"Nigga, ain't nobody tryna pin a seed on nobody. You broke now anyways. Everybody done already heard of how Jayce played your ass. Shit, I wish it was his baby. From what I know, his ass rolling in dough," she said, chuckling. I couldn't even be mad at this bitch.

"Holla at me in nine months, so we can take this paternity test. Tee, don't come back around here no more," I said while raising up out my seat and walking over to the door and opening it to let her out.

I looked outside to see if Honesty was still around, but she wasn't. I had no clue where she went and how she got there, and a nigga would be lying if he said that I aint wanna go out there and find her.

"See you in nine months," Tiana sang into my ear as she walked past me, making sure her ass brushed against my dick.

I slammed the door behind her and locked it before sitting my ass down. I rolled up a big spliff and grabbed a bottle of Henny. This shit was much needed. A nigga needed to escape, and it seemed like I couldn't catch a break. Everything was hitting me all at once, and the main thing on my mind was how I was going to make this money and Honesty. I wanted her to give me a good reason on why she did what she did. Not even why she did it but more so why she didn't tell me. She didn't know how much shit could've been avoided had she let a nigga know. There was nothing I wouldn't do for her, and I had proved that time and time again. But it seemed like she was living in her past... like if she was still in survival mode. I shook my head and smoked my blunt until it went out. I needed the day to myself, and tomorrow, I was going to get back to business.

Honesty

The look on Ahmad's face was the only image that played in my head, and it was impossible to get it out. He looked as if I had stolen from him, but I knew that was not the case. My stealing was what had him in the predicament he was in. I was stupid and selfish and should've told him, but I didn't. I couldn't even go back and look at him. I was ashamed, ashamed of him and that bitch Tiana. I refused to let her see me act a fool. The only time she was allowed to see me show my ass was when I was on top of her, beating that ass. Other than that, my pride wouldn't let me. I left with my dignity and pride, and he ripped my heart out the minute she announced she was pregnant. I knew that dirty bitch was trying to get under my skin, but there was nothing I could do or say to Ahmad to make him open his eyes and see that. I lied to him so much that I knew he didn't believe I was capable of telling the truth. Even telling him I was pregnant made me sound like a fool. What proof did I have?

I lay on Naomi's bed and cried my eyes out; this shit had become a routine for me. I had laid here for three days straight only getting up to pee. Ms. G was forcing me to eat. She was still happy about being a grandma. I couldn't muster up the strength to tell her it wasn't happening. I didn't deserve to be a mother. I was too selfish and nothing like my mother. She had been nothing but selfless. In a few hours, the life that was growing in me would be gone. This little life had been made of love, the love that Ahmad and I shared that I had fucked up. He didn't love me anymore, and that was all I wanted. His love was the only thing that could mend my broken heart. The thought of how we once were so happy, and the fact that we weren't was all my fault. It made my chest hurt so bad. The pain was so unbearable that someday I felt like my heart itself would stop beating. I had lost my mom, Nay, and Ahmad, the one person that I could've prevented from leaving me had I been honest, but I wasn't. My name didn't fit me at all. Why couldn't she have named me Hannah instead? I was a fraud, and I didn't need anyone to tell me what I already knew.

I threw on a Pink sweat suit and my Ones and rushed out the door without saying a word. I had to get this baby out of me. I got on the bus and headed straight to the abortion clinic. I couldn't raise a fatherless child and refused to. My mother struggled with Hannah and I, and I had always vowed that I wouldn't do the same. I couldn't do the same. I commended my mother for what she did for Hannah and I, but I wasn't strong enough. On the ride to the clinic, I spotted Tiana and Ahmad with her son, and my stomach just gave out on me as I began vomiting on the bus. The tears began falling down on their own. My first heartbreak was one for the books. I couldn't believe this was happening to me. They looked like the perfect little family, and I was nothing, just nothing when I was once his everything.

About thirty minutes later, I was there. I walked inside and a hollow feeling washed over me, but I had to push through. I walked to the counter, and the receptionist looked up and flashed a smile. But what was she smiling for? Did she not know where she was working? Nothing worth smiling about was going on here.

"Hey. Can I have your name?"

"Honesty Harris," I whispered.

The waiting room wasn't crowded, but there were a few little black girls like myself waiting in line to end a life. I could only imagine what all of their stories were—one-night stands, deadbeat daddies, couldn't afford a kid. Shit, everyone had their own story to tell, and who was anyone to judge?

"Oh, you're early," she stated, getting up out her chair and coming around to open the door.

"Follow me this way," she added all while still smiling.

I wanted to slap the smile clean off her face. But just because I was miserable didn't mean she had to be. She led me into a cold, white room and passed me a hospital gown.

"Undress from the bottom down, and the doctor will be in with you shortly," she stated before walking out the room.

I did as I was told and put the gown on before lying down. The tears began to form in my eyes. I just wanted to make this moment go away and move on with my life.

I heard a light knock on the door before the doctor walked in.

"Honesty Harris?" she questioned, and I nodded my head. "Do you know how far along you are?" she asked.

"No. Just get this baby out, please. I would like to be unconscious," I said, not wanting to talk any further. She nodded her head and gave me a needle.

"Count down from one hundred," she said.

The tears began rushing out my eyes as I counted. "Ninety-nine, ninety-eight, ninety-seven…" Before I knew it, I was out like a light.

I woke up in a different room with a bright light in my face, and all I could do was lean over the side of my bed and vomit. I couldn't believe it. Just like that, the baby was gone. I didn't know how long it had been since I was knocked out, but it felt like it had been a whole day. I vomited, and the tears rushed out my eyes. I was feeling weak, and the only thing I could do was vomit. The thought of no baby made me cry even harder. Just a few days ago, I wondered if the baby would look like Ahmad or like me, and suddenly, there was no one there. It was something we wouldn't find out. Every inch of pain I felt physically and emotionally, I deserved it all. I didn't feel bad for myself, and I didn't want anyone to feel bad for me. I had made my bed, and I had to lie in it. I had something good and fucked it all up for nothing.

I rose up out the bed and looked for my clothes. Even though I was a little dizzy, I was ready to go. Being in here reminded me of what had just happened, and I didn't want to be reminded. I got dressed and walked out, wishing that I had money for a cab. Shit, I didn't even have a phone let alone money for a cab. I began walking to a bus station, and the area I was in looked familiar, but I couldn't pinpoint it. I looked around, trying to remember. I walked a few blocks down and realized I was right in front of Lorraine's. I was dizzy and still nauseous, and everything in me told me turn around go back to the bus station, and the part of me that didn't listen, the part of me that hadn't told Ahmad the truth told me to go see if I could find Nay. Somehow, between trying to figure out what I was going to do, I passed out.

* * *

I HAD no idea how long I had been out for, but my head was on a thousand, and I figured it was from hitting my head on concrete. I felt the weight of someone's body on top of mine, and before things could become clear to me, I realized that I was being raped and knew exactly where I was. I was in Trick's bando. My body was fully exposed for the world to see, and I began to panic. I used all the strength I could muster up and kick whoever was on top of me in the nuts. I thought the nigga would fall over in pain, but he didn't. He wrapped his hand around my neck and continued to thrust.

I could feel wetness in between my legs, and I knew it wasn't from me being wet, but from the blood of the abortion. I began to try to fight him off, but I just stopped. Maybe this was my karma. I deserved this pain. I lay still and stiff, letting this unknown man have his way with me. No tears could fall. I had cried all my tears. I was at my breaking point. It was only so much a girl could take.

After nutting all over my stomach, he rose up and walked away. I felt dirty. Maybe this was where I belonged. I lay still and watched as men came up to me, saw the blood everywhere, and walked away. A part of me was relieved, and a part of me was ashamed and disgusted with myself.

After lying there deep in my own thoughts for a few hours, I heard Naomi.

"Honesty, that you? Let's get you cleaned up, girl."

I sat up slowly and looked ahead of me, and just as I thought, it was a sober Naomi. Any other time, I would've been happy to see her, but the look on my face held no emotion. She had lost some weight since the last time I had seen her, and from the track marks on her arm, I could tell she had been shooting up. I felt just as bad for her as I felt for myself. What I felt for her was worst, though. She had no idea about the life Trick was introducing her to, and that was what made me hate him for her. She grabbed my hand and led me to the bathroom.

"Get yourself cleaned up. I'll go find your clothes," she said before walking out.

I looked into the bathroom mirror. Nothing but disappointment plagued my face. I had done this to myself. I just couldn't believe that I had played myself like this. I turned on the sink and grabbed a handful of paper towels and took a hoe bath. The bleeding in between my legs hadn't stopped, and I had dried up blood all over the lower half of my body. Just as I had gotten cleaned up, Nay was back with my clothes and a pad. I had no idea where the hell she managed to find not only my shit but a pad as well, but I wasn't going to ask. I was happy as shit I didn't have to walk around naked. I began to get dress, and she pulled out some coke and began making lines. I didn't protest or try to talk her out of it. This was her lifestyle, and who was I to judge? I sat beside her and watched her in between tears as she snorted two lines. It seemed like I had no control over my emotions at that point. The tears fell whenever they felt like it, and I was tired of trying to stop them. It did nothing but cause me more pain.

"You know I ain't gon' peer pressure you, but if you wanna try it, it's here. You look like you could use it, ole emotional ass," she said with a slight smile, sounding a little bit like her regular self.

She sat the tray down and walked over to the sink, and I stared hard and long before picking it up and sniffing a line. This was my "What could possibly go wrong?" moment. And I just needed to feel something other than what I was feeling. A tingling, warm, and calm sensation came over me, and all I could think was *finally, a peace of mind.*

I put my head back against the wall in a nod and let the high take me to another place. I needed to escape, and this drug was the plane that was taking me to cloud nine.

Ahmad

"*Noooo! I'm not leaving! I'm pregnant.*"

I opened my eyes from the rest I was trying to get, but it seemed like every time I closed my eyes, I saw and heard her. I looked at the unlit blunt in my hand and put it in the ashtray. My life had gone to left field since the day I put her out, and a nigga was in the dark. Syd and Kai stayed true to they word, and every day, there was bodies dropping whether it was their men or mine. NYC had no idea what the fuck they were getting hit with. My niggas had even been retaliating and traveling to Brooklyn to make some bloodshed. I had been on the move, trying to get money the one other way I knew how, and that was gambling. I had become a regular at the casino. In three weeks, I had doubled up the money, so to me, that was progress. I rose up off the couch, which had become my new bed. A nigga couldn't even rest in the bedroom because everything smelled just like her. That shit was unhealthy. I looked at her phone on the table and picked it up. No missed calls. I was regretting my choice every day and living with the pain behind my decision. We could've worked it out, but I was so blinded with anger that I didn't want to. I had literally scared her away. She hadn't called or came around. I thought maybe she would, but that wasn't happening. I pulled my wife beater over my head and got low to the floor and started doing push-ups. Working out and the weed was the only thing that cleared my mind. My body muscle was definitely more defined. I worked out until my body gave out. Drenched in sweat, I got up off the floor and went straight to the shower.

About ten minutes later, I was out and dressed. I walked over to the couch and grabbed my phone. I had two missed calls. They weren't from who I wanted them to be from. It was Tiana. She couldn't understand what nine months meant. She was always hitting a nigga up and needing shit. I came through because of the .5 percent possibility of her being my child's mother. Once I knew for sure that she wasn't, I'd wash my hands of her. So whatever she needed, I tried to help out with. I didn't know if she took my kind gestures as we were going to fuck around again, but if that was what she had in mind, she had it all fucked up. A nigga's heart was bleeding for one person and one person only, and she wasn't it.

I shook my head and put my phone in my pocket. Enough was enough. I was going to go get my lady. I had let my pride and ego take over for too long. I wasn't going to try to do this thing where I had to live without her. She brought out a side of me that I was incapable of showing another woman. No other woman made my heart feel like it would fall out my chest. This shit was some life or death pain, and I wasn't ready to find out what death was like. So if I was going to live this life, it was going to be with her.

I grabbed her phone off the table and my car keys and headed to the door. Shit was déjà vu when I opened it up. There stood Tee with Quan in her arms and two bulky ass suitcases. I didn't know what had her feeling so comfortable to a point where she thought she could just pop up. I wasn't up for the bullshit. I was on a mission, so I was hoping she was going to make it quick.

"What are you doing here?" I asked in a flat tone.

"If you would've answered your phone or even listened to your voicemail, you would know that I need a place to stay. I was evicted."

I looked at her, wanting to say that wasn't my problem, but that small percentage of her carrying my child wouldn't allow me to do that.

"Bruh, your rent is like five dollars. You couldn't keep up with that? Shit, you ask me to do every other got damn thing else. You couldn't ask me to loan you money for rent Tee? This some bullshit."

I was beyond annoyed with her at that point. I knew I couldn't just leave her dumbass just out here on the porch or homeless. I rubbed my hand over my hair and opened the door for her to bring her things in.

"I'm going out, and I damn sure ain't leaving you in my house by yourself, so let's go, " I said.

I didn't trust Tiana, and it wasn't no secret. I was dreading even letting her stay with me. I stood by the door waiting for her to walk out with her son. I locked the door and unlocked the car, and of course, this bitch thought she was about to have her son riding in the back seat by himself with no car seat.

"I'm not even about to do this with you. Get in the back seat with him, or you can wait on the porch until I get back."

I got in, and she stood outside the car with her arms folded, trying to pout, but it just looked sour.

She didn't realize that nothing that had to do with her feelings moved me. I started up the car, and that got her ass to jump right in the back with him. Everything in me wanted her to act a fool, so she would have to sit outside until I got back. I shrugged her off and headed toward Ms. G's crib.

* * *

"WHO IS IT?" I heard Hannah ask from the other end of the door.

"Ahmad." The door unlocked quickly, and she jumped on me, giving me a hug.

"Oh my god, Ahmad! I've missed you! Are you here to pick me up for the weekend? Where's Honesty?" she asked all in one breath while letting me in. Her question confused me but also made my stomach knot up.

"Lil' boss, not this weekend. Next weekend, I'll be by to get you. Your sister isn't here?" I asked, following her into the kitchen. I walked over to the elder and gave her a hug.

"No, baby. She was here for days, crying and starving herself, but I wasn't having it, especially since she pregnant. It was just all so unhealthy. I figured y'all made up the way she dashed up out this house," Ms. G replied.

Her words hit me like a ton of bricks. The look of shock on my face caused her to continue talking.

"Oh, baby, she didn't tell you yet? Shit! Act surprised when she does. 'Cause it ain't my place."

I was at lost for words. I nodded my head and headed back toward the door and out the building. When I got to the car, Tiana was standing outside, leaning on the door and talking to one of the niggas on the block.

I got in the car and started it up, and she jumped right in before I could drive off.

I didn't know where I was going, but I had to find Honesty. I couldn't believe that she was really pregnant. I thought she had just said that so that I wouldn't put her out. Tears threatened to fall from my eyes as I sped down the block. I wasn't going to sleep until I found her. What was better than one set of eyes? A dozen. I shot Big Mike a picture of Honesty and a message.

Me: *Anybody sees her, call my jack. I need every eye and ear out looking for her.*

Honesty

"Why yo' ass never told me getting high felt this good?" I asked Nay as we sat in our usual spot in the bathroom doing our lines.

I was no longer stressed out. I was living life, and when I was high, I was happy. I thought of Ahmad every day, but the thought of him took me to a dark place, a place that I never wanted to be, so I had managed to push him so far in the back of my head that I would sometimes even forget what he looked like and smelled like. I wasn't sure if it was a good or bad thing, but it kept me sane.

"Bitch, cause yo' ass be tripping. Shit, the way I feel when I'm high. ain't nothing that I could explain to you without looking like a fiend. It's just some shit you gotta see for yourself," she said as she caressed her body in the mirror.

Being in the bando was cool and all. It was a life I learned to accept. I couldn't have Ahmad in my life, but I had someone who understood me, and that was Nay. She understood the ups the downs, the trials and tribulations, and I didn't have to cover shit up for her. She had chosen this life because of a man. I had run to this life to escape a man. Shit, if you asked me, men were the root of all evil. Them motherfuckers came into your life, made you feel all good about yourself. and spoiled you, and right when they got you where they wanted you, it was like a switch flipped in their little brains, and they turned into someone you couldn't even recognize.

I remember Naomi being all happy, giddy, and head over heels over Trick's trifling ass because he was buying her the latest designer and spoiling her. But I knew a snake when I saw one, and Trick's ass was as sneaky as they come. All that shit, in the beginning, was just a façade for the real deal. He lured women in by catering to their every need so they could cater to his, then drugged them up and had them start tricking for him. From what I understood, the start of tricking wasn't the bad part. It was the part where he got you so hooked on drugs that your ass was not tricking for Chanel and Gucci, but you were tricking for that bag of white powder. It had taken Naomi some time to figure out that Trick didn't want her.

In the month I had been here, I seen her fight about four women and even attack Trick. Shit, that day was a day for everybody to remember. He didn't know who he was messing with. If he thought she was alone, he had another thing coming. She went upside his head with a beer bottle, and he slapped her. I jumped on that nigga back so fast, you would have thought that I had springs beneath my feet. I clawed at his eyes, but it wasn't too long before he beat both our asses.

If you asked me, that was the day Nay and I made a name for ourselves because we had done the unthinkable. We had done what every girl in here wanted to do, but they were scared. Although we were in pain and all lumped up, looking like Martin Lawrence, Nay and I found that shit funny. It was just like old times, sitting down with one another and laughing at dumb shit. I mean, our circumstances were way different, but shit, the one thing that remained the same was that we had each other.

I stood beside her in the mirror, and I had definitely loss that baby weight. I was smaller than Hannah at that point, but I was happy to be alive.

"Let's go start some shit," Naomi said as she ran her fingers through her hair. If we took care of anything in here, it was our hygiene and hair. The type of hoe baths we took made people question if there was a hidden shower somewhere. We were washing our asses like we were at home. When our clothes needed to be changed, Trick came by with the old shit that the new girls were tired of wearing and let us have them. Shit, even though we were at the bottom of the barrel when it came to his food chain, Nay and I had the best clientele. Niggas would line up waiting for us to fuck them, so we used that to our advantage. Trick didn't hold anyone hostage. We were free to come and go as we pleased. But any time Nay and I threatened to get clean and walk away from this shit hole, he did exactly what we asked.

A knock on the bathroom door made Nay and I turn toward it, and speaking of the devil, there stood Trick.

"Hey, daddy's little money makers. I got a client for the both of y'all," he said, flashing that ugly smile of his.

I didn't know what it was that attracted Nay to him, but I couldn't see it. Maybe all she could see before was dollar signs.

"What they paying?" I said with an attitude. He held up two baggies of white powder. I threw my hair in a ponytail and snatched a bag from him, leaving the other one for Nay.

"We need to talk," she said to him with her arms crossed across her chest.

"We will talk after your client leaves," he said, tossing her the bag in disgust and just walking away. She caught it, and we both squealed before putting them in our bras.

"Bet you I get this nigga to cum in five minutes," I challenged.

"Bitch, watch me be done in three," she retorted, and just like that, we made fun out of our lives.

Life wasn't that bad. We weren't dependent on anyone except ourselves, and we wouldn't let one another down. We hadn't. I walked out, and two men in their mid-fifties stood waiting for us.

"I got dibs on the fat boy. They tire out fast," I said, cracking a joke and speed walking over to him.

He groped my butt and tried to kiss me, but I turned my head. That was not what we were here for, and I'd be damned if I let his greasy old ass put his mouth on me. I pushed him onto the bed, and he pulled down his pants. I went to throw a condom on so I could throw the pussy at him, but he objected.

"I just wanna see what that mouth do," he said. I looked down at his uncircumcised penis and gagged.

Nay burst out in laughter while riding the other man's dick. I held my breath and did my two-hand twist jerking off movement on him and added some spit on top. I refused to put my mouth on this man. He was so damn big he couldn't see what I was doing because his big ass belly was in the way. I used this to my advantage and went faster and faster. Before I knew it, he was cumming, and it erupted on my hand. I rose up and ran to the bathroom to wash my hands.

"Fat greaseball, stink motherfucker," I whispered to myself. The fucking audacity. I splashed water on my face and walked out the bathroom and out the new place I called home.

* * *

I TOOK a walk around the block to calm down, and just as I was about to walk back into the bando, I felt a strong arm spin me around. Before I could even look up, the smell that I could never forget invaded my nose. It was him—Ahmad in the flesh. I looked up at him, and my breath got caught in my throat.

"Please, tell me you not doing what the fuck I think you doing!" he said, loud enough for me to hear and aggressive enough for me to know he was pissed.

I put my head down to avoid eye contact and hide the shame that I felt. He had never looked better. He looked like he was living life and living better than he ever did when I was around. It felt like I hadn't seen him in ages. And that feeling that my heart felt came back. It was pumping hard and fierce. I wanted to jump back in his arms and let him take me away from this.

"Come home, ma. I'll get you cleaned up. This ain't you. I'm sorry."

That was all he had to say before I threw my head into his chest and burst out in tears. He held me in his arms, and I held him tightly as if he would disappear right where he stood. He walked with me hand in hand toward the car, and when I finally got close enough, I let go of his hand. Tiana was sitting in the front seat with her legs kicked up and a smirk on her face. To say I was embarrassed was the least. Was he playing house with this bitch? He had put me out and taken her in, and she was pregnant.

My thoughts became too much for my head as I turned around and ran back into the warehouse. I ran head first into Trick, and he was confused until he saw Ahmad come in right behind me. I stood up and stood behind Trick.

"Tell him to go," I said to him loud enough so Ahmad could hear.

I could see that this had become amusing for him. He flashed Ahmad a smile and threw his hands up.

"You heard the lady. She wants to stay with daddy," he said, pulling me closer to him and resting his hand on my hips.

"Honesty, let's go!" Ahmad yelled, causing me to jump.

I wanted to run to him, but my feet stayed glued onto the ground. I couldn't go back to him. It wouldn't be the same. He had moved on and had a family to look out for, and I was nothing but baggage. I refused to be his baggage anymore. I could walk out this place and be good with him for a few months. Something would happen, and I'd be right back at square—one on my ass. I wasn't having it. Plus, the thought of him being with Tiana ate me up.

"No. I'm staying here with daddy," I said.

It had never been so hard to say something in my life as hard as it was to say those words. I would have said anything to get him to go and leave me alone. He shook his head and walked out without another word. My chest was heaving up and down.

"You calling me daddy now?" Trick said while rubbing his dick print on me.

I pushed him in the chest and ran off into the bathroom. I felt like I would die from the anxiety I felt. I grabbed a tray from the bathroom and poured some coke on it and sniffed a line. And just like I thought it would, my heart rate began to slow down. I was getting calm, but my emotions were all over the place. The tears fell down my face as I sat on the floor in the corner. I felt lonely once again. I had escaped feeling this way for so long, and it was back. Right when I thought life was going good, some-thing had to come along and fuck It up.

Ahmad

Six Months Later

I sat outside Ms. G's house waiting for Hannah to come downstairs. I had kept my word, and every weekend, I was coming to pick her up. She insisted on still coming over just in case Honesty came back for her. She'd be on the same schedule she was always on, and I let her. In my head, I knew Honesty was too far gone to ever come back for her sister, but I couldn't tell her that. The last time I had seen her replayed in my mind time and time again, reminding me that had I been rational, I could've avoided all this. It ate a nigga up inside, but I knew she would find her way back with time. The life she was living wasn't hers. But every time I told myself that just maybe she would get tired of living the way she was, more time went by. I had thought constantly of going in there and snatching her up, but I knew firsthand that if someone wasn't ready to get clean, they wouldn't get clean. It had to be something they woke up and decided it was time for them to do.

A dramatic sigh came from Tiana's lips, and I looked over at her with a grill on my face. She and her son were still staying at the crib, and it was hell. The bitch was dirtying up everything and not cleaning up after herself. I was coming in and having to pick up dirty clothes and socks. I was just ready for her to pop, so we could do this DNA test, and she could be out a nigga's life for good. Every minute that Honesty was away, she was trying to fill her shoes. What she didn't know was that she couldn't compete where she didn't compare.

Honesty was my rib, a breath of fresh air, the only person I would lay down and die for. But Tee couldn't understand that. She thought sex was everything. Yeah, I had been fucking her throughout the months. Shit, what harm could it really do? A nigga needed to let his nut off and all that pent up anger and frustration that I had accumulated in the past few months.

"Oh my God! Where is that fucking brat?" she said while sucking her teeth and putting her feet up on my dashboard.

I was about sick of this shit. I had constantly told the bitch stop putting her funky fungus filled toes on my shit, but talking to her was like talking to a brick wall.

"Watch your fucking mouth. It ain't nothing for you to get the fuck out. And take your feet off my shit. I'm not gon tell you again Tee," I replied in a serious tone.

I had made it clear to her in the past to not speak about Honesty or say anything to Hannah, two lines she couldn't cross. I had to scold her more than she scolded her damn son. That shit was ridiculous. I didn't know how niggas had multiple baby's mothers. The possibility of one alone was driving me up a fucking wall. She pouted and put her foot down and crossed her arms, and like a light switch, her mood changed.

"I'm sorry, baby. It's just these hormones," she said, leaning over the center console and rubbing my dick through my pants and trying to get close to my face. I turned my head, and like clockwork, Hannah jumped in the car.

"Sorry I took so long, I was pulling out the weeds," she said closing the door behind her.

"You know if you would've told me, I would come and help you," I said in a joking tone. "Mess around and pull out one of Ms. G's vegetables," I added while chuckling. Hannah began to laugh also.

"Yeah, okay. Like the last time. And try to blame it on me again?"

I chuckled at the memory. I had been taking care of Hannah how I knew Honesty would if she was off that shit. Ms. G could only do so much. Even though she tried to act like she wasn't worried about Honesty and Naomi, I knew she was. Every time there was a knock on the door, she added a little more pep in her step just in case one of them came to their senses. The way she hoped they came home, I used to hope, but that hope faded away for me.

"Where you trying to go, lil' boss?" I asked while pulling off.

"Um, let's go to the Barnes and Nobles in Harlem," she suggested.

She had chosen Harlem specifically because she hoped to run into Honesty and be the reason she came home. She didn't know that I knew that was the reason she wanted to go there, but I didn't say a word. I just turned the music up and was on my way. When we got to Barnes and Nobles, we filed out the car.

Tiana's ass started complaining. "A fucking bookstore? We spending our time at a fucking bookstore? Is there a mall or something around here? Shit, I'll walk if I have to."

Hannah began to chuckle before speaking up. "Yeah, a bookstore. Maybe you could learn something or teach your son something like his numbers and colors. Shit, he barely talk as it is."

Tiana's mouth dropped open like she was shocked at what Hannah said, and she looked over at me to see if I'd say anything, but I didn't. Hannah had hit the nail right on the head. Quan had just turned three and wasn't doing as much talking as the average three-year-old, and Tiana wasn't the least bit worried. She was steady worried about getting money out of me for dumb shit like Gucci diaper bags and Fendi strollers that she couldn't even see that her child was delayed.

I shook my head and walked into the bookstore and over to the section where they held criminal law books, and Hannah went to American Lit. We both scanned until we found a book that interested us and sat in our usual secluded spot by one of the big windows, which we both took glances out of every now and again, thinking that there was a chance we'd see her. I wondered if Honesty even knew how much we wanted her to come home or if she even wanted to. I had figured that if she wanted to, she'd be home, but nah, something had to give. The love we shared wasn't fake, and I knew if my heart ached at the mere thought of her, she had to feel the same way too, right? Or was I bugging? This love shit was confusing, and if I couldn't have Honesty, I knew I wouldn't love again. This shit hurt more than a bullet wound. I opened my book and began to read.

"Why every time we come here, you reading about criminal law? Shit, I know good and well you ain't going to law school, so what's the deal?" Hannah asked while putting her book down, and I chuckled.

"Well, at least we on the same page about not going to law school, but what's wrong with trying to have knowledge on it when I'm breaking it?" I asked without taking my eyes off the book in front of me.

"Hmm… You might be on to something. Where your little girlfriend anyways? You think I scared her off?" she asked with a giggle and looked around the store.

I looked up at her and laughed. She was definitely Honesty's sister. She wasn't as aggressive, but that passive aggressive shit was what she was good at, and she got under Tee's skin when she did it.

"I wish. I'm pretty sure you set her straight. She somewhere around here with a book."

"Or magazine," she added, and I chuckled.

"When Honesty comes home, can we all move away somewhere? I say Florida maybe. I've had enough of New York City," she said with a shrug.

I closed my book, because obviously, Hannah didn't come here to read. She had come here to talk and hope that Honesty strolled by.

"That don't sound too bad. Why Florida?" I asked, not thinking that I'd get any real answer.

She looked out the window and scanned the crowd of people before speaking up again.

"Florida is where we begged our mom to move before she got cancer, and she told us if she beat it the last time we would go."

Her voice cracked a bit, and I didn't want her getting all emotional on me. Hannah and I had built a bond and a relationship that no longer revolved around Honesty. She was really like the little sister I never had, and I was okay with that.

"Come on. Let's go find Ursula, so we can head home and order some food," I suggested while standing up.

She nodded her head, and we walked around the store looking for her. I received a text message, and it was an image of Hannah with a red dot on her chest and a money symbol. I knew exactly who it was coming from, and my heart raced. I grabbed her arm and rushed to the car while dialing Tiana's number. She let the phone go to voicemail, and I dialed her again. Hannah could sense my urgency and put some pep in her step. Tiana answered right before it went to voicemail.

"I'm going around the block. Meet me outside," I said while jumping in the car and pulling off.

I didn't want to just sit out front waiting on her like a sitting duck, so I drove around the block, and when I got back in front of Barnes and Noble, for the first time, Tiana had actually listened to what I told her to do. She jumped in the car, and I sped down the busy city streets while looking in my rearview and side mirrors to see if I was being followed. After I was sure I wasn't, I drove straight to the house. That was a warning text from Syd and Kai about their money.

I had managed to flip the money and make more than what I owed them without any connect or plug, but they had added interest and doubled the payment, so I owed them bitches a mil. I wasn't going to just give them everything and be left with nothing. I had their half a mil, but they were trying to make an example out of me. I had to think of something and fast.

I got to the house and went straight into my office and dialed Big Mike. "Boss, the block is hot. Bloodshed everywhere! Them pigs is crawling, trying to figure out what the fuck is going on. I'mma lay low, and you do the same," he said frantically before hanging up.

I knew that this meant that Syd and Kai were coming for me next. I sat at my desk and called in a favor from someone I trusted that owed me their life. It was time to pay their debt.

"Ty'shawn Grey residence. May I ask whose speaking?" a woman answered.

"Can you tell him it's Ahmad? It's urgent." The city wasn't safe no more, and it was time to really get low.

"Hello, Ahmad," I heard a deep voice say into the phone.

"Wassup, Pops? I'm calling to cash in that favor. I need to be on the first thing out of here undetected," I said, cutting straight to the chase.

"Aight, son. The earliest I can get you out of here is tomorrow at noon. I'll send a car to your place," he replied, and what other choice did I have? I just had to lay low for a few more hours, and then I'd be up out of here.

"Aight. Good looking."

"Do you need my help with anything else? I know I haven't been much of a father to you, but I still got connections around the city. Stop forgetting your bloodline holds weight in these streets," he began.

"I'm good, Pops. Thanks," I said before hanging up.

My father was Ty'shawn Grey, one of the greatest kingpins to walk the New York streets. He was a married man who fell in love with his mistress. When he was ready to leave his wife for my mother, she went batshit crazy. She let them live their lives and disappeared with her children, but I guess after seeing how happy he was living on a daily with my mother and I, she decided to come back one day and kill my mother. I washed my hands of him. The minute I turned eighteen, I was out the house and on my own.

I could have just told him about the problem with Syd and Kai and have him make it go away, but I didn't want to do that. I was a man, and I was going to face them one day. Just not this day because they were being irrational and trying to just make an example out of me.

I walked out the office and down the stairs. Tiana was sitting on the couch watching ratchet TV with Quan on her lap, and Hannah was in the kitchen cooking. I walked into the kitchen and took a seat at the island. I didn't know what other way to tell Hannah this without beating around the bush.

"How about we leave for Florida tomorrow?"

She spun around with a huge smile on her face, but when she realized what I'd just said, the smile wiped off her face.

"No, Ahmad. We can't leave Honesty. I'm all she has, and she's all I have. We can't leave her," she said with tears in her eyes threatening to fall.

I knew this wasn't gonna be easy for her, but I also knew it wasn't safe out here anymore.

"Hannah, Honesty is in a bad place, but she is safe where she is, and we aren't. We can just go for a while and come back after her when things cool down." I tried to negotiate with her. I knew whether she agreed or not, we had to get the hell up out New York if we didn't want to take a dirt nap.

"Promise that we'll come back for her," she demanded, and it was a promise I had no problem making.

"I promise," I said, twisting my pinky fingers into hers. It was something she had taught me every time I promised. Shit, if I didn't know how serious a promise was before, I knew because of that.

I walked into the living room and turned off the TV.

DAK

"Tee go pack some things up. We taking a trip." She jumped up and squealed in excitement.

"Oh my God! Really, Ahmad! Oh, let me go pack up some stuff! Where we going?" she questioned, and I shook my head.

She was due any day, and I just couldn't wait. She needed to have that baby not now but right now. I walked away from her and into my bedroom. I grabbed a small suitcase that I used for business meetings and backed a few things inside. I would buy everything once we got to Florida, so I was trying to pack lightly. I grabbed Jay's chain and put it in the bottom of my bag along with a picture of Honesty and I at her birthday party. I looked at the picture one time before shaking my head and putting my basic necessities in the bag. I closed it up and put it downstairs. I noticed that Hannah had dinner ready and the table set up for us all.

"I wasn't gonna set the table, but I might as well since it'll be the last dinner in here. I spoke with Ms. G and just told her we were taking a trip," she said from behind me.

I washed my hands and took a seat, and so did she. I didn't know any fifteen-year-old that could throw down like Hannah. She cooked better than Honesty, and that I could vouch for. We sat at the table and waited for Tiana and Quan. Five minutes later, she was coming down with him in her arms.

"You know he can walk, right? Carrying him and that belly can't be comfortable," Hannah said.

"Little girl, this is my child. If I wanna carry him on top of my head 'til he's thirty, I can do that. Don't worry about him," she snapped back. I had too much on my mind to deal with a nagging little sister and baby mama. She sat Quan in the seat and went to reach for a bowl. Like it was an instinct, Hannah popped her on the hand and scrunched up her face.

"You and yo' son need to wash y'all hands, and we say grace before eating."

"Ahmad, this little girl put her hands on me again. I won't care about being homeless. I'll break all her fingers off," Tiana said, redirecting her energy to me. I wasn't moved by her threat.

"I'd like to see you try it," Hannah replied, standing up and sizing her up. The two glared at one another before Tiana snatched her son's hand up and went to wash them.

118

When she returned to the table, we all bowed our heads while Hannah began saying grace.

"Father God, I would like to thank you so much for providing us with this food for our bellies. I would also like to thank you for giving us all some sense enough to remember to say our daily grace. Last but not least, please bring Honesty home. Amen."

"Amen," I said after her, and she turned her face toward Tiana, waiting for her to say it.

"Amen," Quan said, and it shocked us all.

He rarely spoke, so when he did, it was a surprise. This changed Tiana's whole mood, and she finally said Amen. We passed around the bowl of goulash and garlic bread and ate like we hadn't eaten all day. We didn't always get along, but good food could always bring people together.

* * *

THE NEXT MORNING couldn't come soon enough. I had barely gotten any sleep. I took the saying "sleep with one eye open" to the next level because that was exactly what I did. My nerves were on edge. All we had to do was wait a couple more hours, and we'd be out of here. I walked into the kitchen, and Hannah was at the table eating a breakfast that she had made. She had left a plate for Tiana and I. Tiana couldn't see it, but she was harmless. Although she picked at her, she still made sure to make enough food for her and her son.

I looked at both plates filled with eggs, bacon, and toast and grabbed the one that had least on it, knowing Tiana would share hers with her son. Every day, she began to look more and more like Honesty. And from the way she was checking Tiana, she was growing into that attitude of hers. I just wished that Honesty could see how much she had matured and grown from the last time she saw her. But I knew her vision was clouded, and what I saw, she could never see.

"I miss Honesty. I can't understand why she just won't come home," Hannah said, putting her fork down. I took a deep breath. What she wanted was what I wanted, but it was a want that we couldn't have.

"It's easy for us to say for her to come home, but it's not easy for her to actually come," I explained while putting a forkful of food in my mouth.

Before Hannah could respond, a call came through to my phone from an unknown number. Everything in me wanted to not answer it, but as if it had a mind of its own, my hand swiped across the screen and answered it.

"Ahmad?"

I heard Honesty's voice through the phone. Her voice was like music to my ears. My heart began beating like a drum, and no matter how I tried to calm down, I couldn't. Words couldn't even form out my mouth because of how shocked I was.

"Ahmad," she spoke again.

I wanted to reply so badly. I had a million thoughts in my mind, but all I could get out was, "Where are you?"

I grabbed my car keys, got up out the seat, and headed for the front door with Hannah on my tail. My reaction gave it away, and she knew it was her sister.

"Ms. Grandberry's house. Nay's gone."

She sobbed into the phone and was not able to catch her breath. I had heard her cry one other time like that, and that was when her mother died. She had taken L after L, and I knew I had to help her.

"Stay there, and I'll be there in a second," I said. I grabbed mine and Hannah's bag and put them in the limo that my father had sent.

I rushed upstairs and grabbed all the money I had made and put it in the car as well. I looked at the driver, and it was the same driver my father had when I was a kid.

"Wassup, Lamine? I have something I need to handle. If I'm not back in time, get Tiana and her son to the airstrip. I'll meet you there." He nodded his head, and I rushed to my car where Hannah was already seated. I did fifty to Ms. G's house.

As I drove, I noticed a black Chevy following me. I knew it was Syd and Kai's people, but it wasn't the time. I tried to drive faster to lose him, but he was right on my ass.

"Hannah, pass me the gun in the glove compartment," I said to her, and her eyes widened in shock.

She had never seen this side of me, and my lifestyle was what had made her run back to Ms. G's place . She knew I was trouble but never knew the extent of how deep in the game a nigga really was. Every sharp turn I made, the Chevy made. I thought of not going to Ms. G's house, but I couldn't risk the fact that Honesty could leave if I didn't get there fast enough. When I was just a block away from Ms. G's house, the car bumped into the back of mine.

"Ahhh!" Hannah screamed. I couldn't blame her. She had no idea what was going on.

"Pass me the gun, Hannah."

With shaky hands, she passed the gun to me while doing a silent prayer.

"I got you, Hannah. I promise," I said, sticking my pinky finger out and letting her twist hers into mine.

When we got in front of Ms. G's house, I saw a young frail woman on the corner. If I would've never made eye contact with her, I would've never known it was Honesty. Those eyes, the eyes that had drawn me into her, were the only thing that remained the same. She had lost a tremendous amount of weight. I was almost sure that baby Quan weighed more than her.

In any other instance, I would've been out the car and picking her up to take her inside, but in that particular scenario, I couldn't. If I stopped, we would all be dead. It wasn't a smart thing to do that when there were goons in the car behind us, and they were most definitely strapped.

"Honesty, get in!" I yelled while letting shots go behind me.

Headshot! I thought as the bullet went straight through the windshield and hit the driver in the head. Honesty ran toward the car, and I watched as another black Chevy tried to pull up in front of me to block me in. But Honesty jumped in just in time, allowing me to speed by, but not before they pulled out their guns and began shooting.

"Duck!" I yelled while pushing Hannah's head down as I tried to shoot out the window.

I tried to take the tires out on the car, so I could lose them, but my luck had ran out. I had no more bullets. I threw the gun down and began to floor it. The only way we were getting out of this was with speed.

Honesty

This felt like something out of a bad movie.

"Ahhhh!" Hannah and I yelled as Ahmad made sharp turns, trying to lose them.

The John who I sliced and stole from had circled the block a few times before Ahmad got here, and I thought I could get into the car before he saw me, but I didn't. I couldn't believe this fat, low-budget Rick Ross was going this hard over a few bills. Maybe it was the anger of me slicing him. Shit, with the way he looked and smelled, I knew he was nobody's boss, but shit, maybe I shouldn't have judged a book by its cover because looks were deceiving. I threw the phone out the window hoping that he would stop the chase, but it didn't end. Instead, more bullets rang out into the car. I kept my head down low as he continued shooting.

I couldn't believe this shit. Where the fuck were the police? Shit, they were always around when you didn't need them, and the one minute every single law was being broken, they were nowhere to be found. Ahmad got onto the freeway, and finally, the gunshots stopped. After about five minutes, I looked out the glassless back windshield, and just as I thought, he'd lost them.

"Oh my God! Thank God he's gone," I said, and then it finally hit me. I was sitting in a car with Hannah and Ahmad.

I hadn't seen them in what felt like years. My stomach got all knotted up because I knew I wasn't looking like what they remembered. I was thinner, and my hair had fallen out because of the lack of care. There was no telling how many people had worn the clothes I had on before me. I was just happy to finally be home. The thought of Nay not making it out caused tears to well in my eyes. It was the same reason I hadn't gone upstairs to Ms. G's house. How could I go upstairs and tell her that I was back but her daughter was dead? She would probably blame me, although we all knew it was no one's fault. But when in a moment of crisis, we all needed someone to blame. I tried to push the thought and image of Nay's dead body out of my mind. I looked over at Ahmad, and he had a look of panic on his face.

"Hannah! No, baby! No!" he yelled, and I looked over at Hannah.

"Ahhhhhh!" I screamed at the top of my lungs.

Her head was slumped, and there was blood everywhere. She couldn't be gone. I had come back for her. There was no way God was doing this to me.

"Stop the car!" I yelled but Ahmad didn't listen. "I said stop the car!" I yelled again with my voice cracking.

I leaned her seat back, so I could see her entire face and just cried over her body. There wasn't a pulse, and I knew it, but I couldn't just let her go without doing CPR. I had remember watching TV and seeing Meredith Grey come back to life. I needed for Hannah to come back. I needed her more than she needed me, and she didn't even know it. I pumped on her chest for about fifteen minutes, and still, there wasn't a pulse. I knew she was gone, but facing it was the hard part. There was no way that she and Nay could just leave me alone in this cold world. I wasn't having it. I wouldn't accept that from them.

I pumped until the car came to a stop at some kind of airstrip, and it was time for me to face the reality of my life. Just like that, I had lost two sisters on the same day. I had failed her. I had done this to her. Who knew me trying to come home would be the death of my sister? I wanted to be better for her, and now, I couldn't. Why couldn't God take me? Hannah had an entire life ahead of her, a life that I never even thought of. She was innocent.

"She's gone, ma," Ahmad said as he picked me up out the car.

NOTE FROM THE AUTHOR

I would like to thank everyone for reading the story of Honesty and Ahmad. Honesty and Ahmad 2 will be coming out soon. I hope you all enjoyed it…

ABOUT THE AUTHOR

My name is Diaka Kaba and I am from the Bronx, NY. I have always had a passion for reading since the third grade. At the time Barbara Parks Junie B. Jones series were godly to me. As I got older picking up The Coldest Winter Ever by Sister Soulja is what got me hooked to Urban fiction. I began writing on Wattpad for fun and I got signed to my first publishing company Shan Presents. When I became a teen mom I put the pen down for a while then realized that every job I worked made me miserable and that writing was my true passion and what made me happy. The author who inspires me the most is Ashley Antoinette. My dream is to one day become New York's Best Selling Author.

Stay Connected:
Email me questions at DIAKASKABA@GMAIL.COM
I will be answering questions about Honesty and Ahmad on my YouTube channel, DAK's Corner.

Royalty Publishing House is now accepting manuscripts from aspiring or experienced urban romance authors!

WHAT MAY PLACE YOU ABOVE THE REST:

Heroes who are the ultimate book bae: strong-willed, maybe a little rough around the edges but willing to risk it all for the woman he loves.

Heroines who are the ultimate match: the girl next door type, not perfect - has her faults but is still a decent person. One who is willing to risk it all for the man she loves.

The rest is up to you! Just be creative, think out of the box, keep it sexy and intriguing!

If you'd like to join the Royal family, send us the first 15K words (60 pages) of your completed manuscript to submissions@royaltypublishing-house.com

LIKE OUR PAGE!

Be sure to <u>LIKE</u> our Royalty Publishing House page on Facebook!

Made in the USA
Middletown, DE
14 March 2019